THE CHRISTMAS COP

BARBARA MCMAHON

1

Shea rubbed her eyes at the same moment her watch vibrated against her wrist. She'd been staring at the computer screen for almost an hour, no wonder her eyes felt dry. Standing, she started walking around the large room, dodging desks and chairs as she made a serpentine circuit. She shook out her hands as she walked, making sure her watch noted the steps.

The Mondano Police Department wasn't known for luxurious accommodations—especially in the work rooms. Lucky for her, this was the overflow office. Though there were six desks and accompanying chairs, no one else used this space. Officers were either in the field or assigned desks in the large bullpen up the hall.

This room was the last stop on the hallway before the holding cells. She'd gotten used to the occasional criminals escorted by the door on their way to the cells. Some muttered, others fought against restraint. Some yelled and others looked dejected. She hadn't seen anyone today.

Stretching, she rotated her shoulders to loosen tight muscles. Checking every line of code for a complex software program wasn't the easiest thing in the world. But she'd find the error and make it right. The reputation of their company was on the line.

When her watch signaled she'd walked enough steps to satisfy the hour, she returned to the desk. It was easier to read the actual code here than the program back at the company. I'd worked on all the demos and all the beta tests. But once actively implemented there was a glitch.

She hated when that happened.

They'd tested and tested over and over to make sure it was flawless. Obviously not tested enough.

Sitting down again in front of the screen, she went back to studying the code—line by line.

When she heard a thumping in the hall, she hardly noticed. Someone else on the way to lockup, she figured.

Only the sound stopped by the door.

Shea glanced up and paused as she observed the man standing there. A cop for sure. She hadn't seen him before—she'd remember. He was tall, with dark hair worn just a little too short for her taste. While he looked mean enough to take on the worst offender, the cane was a dead giveaway that he wasn't going after bad guys any time soon. Her gaze dropped to the left foot, encased in a walking cast.

He stared at her for a long moment.

"I'm Shea O'Riley," she said with a grin.

"What are you doing here? Should you be in this room alone? What are you doing on the computer?" He snapped out the questions.

Shea frowned. So much for a friendly introduction. She withdrew her visitor's badge from her back pocket and flashed it at him.

"Yes, I should be here. Alone suits me and it's none of your business what I'm doing on the computer."

She looked back at the screen and did her best to ignore him. Maybe the police department should give lessons in manners when dealing with non-crooks.

Slowly he walked into the room. From the corner of her eye she saw him studying the layout. Noting more than once his gaze returned to her.

Probably the pink hair.

She'd gotten a lot of notice her first day here from everyone. And not everyone liked pink hair—but she did. At least this month.

Who knew what color would appeal in a few weeks?

He crossed to a desk on the opposite side of the room, as far from her as he could get. He shrugged out of his heavy jacket and draped it over the back of the chair. Then he sat down.

Shea frowned. He wasn't staying, was he? She liked to work alone. Weren't there other desks in the main bull pen he could use? She suspected he was on the disabled list and assigned desk duty. But surely he had a desk he normally used. Unless he was a beat cop. They probably didn't have desks.

A quick glance showed he wasn't the type to welcome desk duty. He looked as if he should be chasing bad guys, maybe even in a gun fight like the marshals in the old west.

He glanced at her and Shea turned her full attention back to the program. As long as he didn't bother her, he could do whatever he wanted.

The office chair he sat in creaked.

She ignored it. And in only moments she was again fully focused on the code.

Jake Morgan carefully laid the cane on the floor. He glared at the desk, the blank computer monitor, the phone. He'd insisted on coming back to work before he was fully fit to return to active duty because of sheer boredom. His broken ankle was healing, but too slowly for him.

It'd been four weeks. At least two or three more to go. And then physical therapy until he could pass the mandated physical to return to duty. The doctor had assured him it'd be off by Christmas, but that was still too long.

Sitting at home with his leg up and nothing to do had about driven him crazy. At least the lieutenant let him return. Though desk duty wasn't something he wanted, he'd make do until he was fully fit again.

At least it got him out of the house.

And cold cases weren't the worst he could have been assigned. He could have been assigned to the public policy department answering questions when people wanted more information on how the Mondano PD worked.

He glanced over at the girl, woman, whatever. She looked like a teenager. Was she playing some game on the computer? Was she related to someone in the building and just killing time?

He took in the short pink hair—cotton candy pink—and wavy around her face. Her eyes were blue. He couldn't accurately judge her height while she was sitting, but suspected she was tall.

Who was she and why was she here?

He turned on the computer, checking the drawers in the desk while he waited for it to boot up. Fully stocked. He knew this room was used by the special task force when a major crime involved more than the Mondano PD. Most of the time it sat vacant.

He didn't know if being here was better than in the main bullpen or worse. There he'd be hearing about investigations and feeling frustrated with lack of involvement. Here, he was totally isolated. He'd do his best on the cold cases, but longed to return to full time duty.

Time would tell if this was better than staying home.

Janey Strobridge walked in, carrying a banker's box.

"Hey, Jake. Good to see you again. How's it going?" she said with a smile.

"I'm doing okay. Those the files?"

"Some of them. There are two more boxes, but I'll let you get through these first."

She put the box on the desk. "Can you manage?"

He nodded. He hated being infirmed. His body couldn't heal fast enough for him.

"Call me if you need anything," she said as she turned to leave.

She glanced at Shea, then looked back at Jake, her eyebrows raised as if questioning how he liked his roommate.

He shrugged and reached out to take the lid off the box.

Drawing out the first thick file folder, he opened it and began to read. It was a murder case that'd never been solved. The dates showed it was almost ten years old. Before he joined the force eight years ago.

He pulled a tablet out of the drawer and began jotting notes.

He was making no headway when, some time later, Shea O'Riley jumped up and began walking around the room.

Distracted, he watched her. He'd been right— she was tall and slender. She sure could fill out a pair of jeans, though.

"Problem?" he asked.

She shook her head, winding her way through the desks.

He watched for another minute.

"What are you doing?"

She flicked him a glance. "Getting steps."

"Huh?"

She kept walking, dodging chairs, turning on a dime and going back.

"My job is very sedentary, I need to make sure I get enough steps in a day to give me some exercise. Sitting for long periods isn't good for you. So I walk."

She looked at her watch. Nodding in satisfaction, she went back to her chair and was soon glued to the screen.

Jake leaned back in his chair. He could use some exercise, but couldn't very well do much with the cast. He'd been elated when he'd been fitted with a walking cast. At least he was more mobile than when he used the crutches. But the limitations still chafed. If he was on his feet too much, his ankle began to ache and took hours to ease.

"I'm Jake Morgan," he said as a belated introduction.

If they were going to share the space for the foreseeable future the least he could do is be polite. It wasn't her fault he didn't want to be looking at cold cases instead of investigating active ones.

She nodded in acknowledgment but didn't look away from the screen.

"It seems like whatever you are looking at is engrossing," he said, curious now to learn what she was doing.

"It's tedious and annoying but yeah, I guess it's engrossing. I'm looking for a glitch in the code for this program."

A computer geek. Who'd have figured?

Though he wondered if pink hair was the norm for those people. He knew basics of computers, but nothing beyond that.

"What program?"

She leaned back in her chair and swiveled around to look at him.

"My company designed a special program for the police to match and tabulate DNA information. Cops started keeping DNA information a long time ago, but there was no standard method to save the data or make it available to others in law enforcement around the country until the National DNA Database. Each county and state can contribute but the protocols differ. This program's designed to draw from all the different databases and conform it to current standards and deliver readable information–to enable it to mesh with Homeland Security's database and cross reference all the other ones out there like FBI and DOJ."

"But there's a glitch?" he repeated.

She nodded. "And I've been here a week and still haven't found it. Of course there's tons of code so I could be here a lot longer. It's just so frustrating. We tested it over and over and it should have worked flawlessly."

"Sounds like an ambitious program. And one that'd help us out a lot."

She nodded. "That's the hope. I guess you got desk duty because of your foot."

"Cold cases, not that I think I'll see anything the officers who initially worked on the cases missed. But my lieutenant thought fresh eyes might spot something. If even one gets solved, I'll be satisfied. Mostly I think it's busy work."

The frustration welled up, but he pushed it away. He knew when he signed on for the job there was the possibility of being injured one day. At least he hadn't been shot.

"Good luck," she said.

"You, too."

When an hour passed, Shea again jumped up and began walking around the room. Jake watched her, amused by her dedication to getting steps. Exercise wasn't something he had to work at normally. Visiting the gym a few times a week kept him in top shape. And the job itself was active enough.

"I'm going out to get lunch, can I bring you something?" Shea asked, returning to her desk and pulling her jacket from the back of her chair. Once on, she reached for a backpack from the knee space of the desk.

He thought he'd make his way to the vending machines and get something. Yet he couldn't resist her offer.

"Where're you going?"

"Ben's Hamburger Joint. It's the closest and I love their fried onion rings."

Jake knew the place, of course. It was a favorite of most cops from the station.

He pulled out his wallet and took a $20 bill, holding it up for her.

"I'll take the double cheeseburger, large fries and a large vanilla milkshake."

She took the money and nodded. "I'll be back soon."

Shea walked through the bullpen to the side door she normally used during business hours. If she worked late, that door was locked and she went through the front. But this one was closer to Ben's and she wanted to get back quickly so the food didn't get cold.

At least Jake Morgan had relented a little to introduce himself. And taken her offer of getting lunch.

He'd been quiet all morning, which helped. If he'd been on the phone all the time, or interviewing people, it'd have proved more difficult to examine the code.

When Shea returned to the office, a bag balanced between drinks in a cardboard carrier, there was another man talking to Jake.

She hesitated at the door, but then entered. It was her space, too.

"There's no one else right now," the man said.

Shea recognized Lieutenant Stephens. Was he Jake's boss?

"Harry retired last spring. He did it for seven years. His files and notes will be there. Mainly it's a liaison job. Make nice to the vendors who donate, match presents with the kids, and arrange for cops to deliver. Piece of cake."

"Not my kind of job," Jake protested.

"With you out of commission, we're short staffed. I need everyone on deck. You can handle it easily from here. You're the best man for the job this year. It won't be a permanent assignment."

"Great," Jake said.

Shea put the lunch on her desk and once she pulled her jacket off, she began to empty the bag of her burger and onion rings.

"I see lunch is here," Lieutenant Stephens said with a smile at Shea. "Janey will bring the files over this afternoon. Since it's already December 3rd, we need to get cracking on it."

"Right," Jake said evenly.

Shea could tell from across the room he wasn't a happy camper about the situation, whatever it was.

When the lieutenant left, she carried Jake's lunch over to his desk. She reached in her pocket and retrieved the change, also putting it on the desk.

"Problem?" she asked.

"Nothing I can get out of," he said, reaching for the double burger. "Thanks for getting this."

"I really like Ben's. I go there almost every day."

They ate in companionable silence. Shea glanced at the computer screen, then away. She needed some time away from the stupid program. Why did it work at their company and not here? They'd trained those who'd be using it. They didn't mess with it, did they?

She hadn't thought about that before.

If so, she hadn't come across any changes yet. So far the code looked solid.

Shea finished lunch and was about to start work again when three cops came in laughing and cracking jokes. One carried another banker's box.

"Hey, if it isn't the Christmas cop," the tall one said.

2

Shea looked from the men to Jake. The other two laughed as they all moved to crowd around his desk. One sat on the side of the desk, his manner totally teasing.

"Finally found a job you can handle," he said placing the box in the middle of the desk on top of the open file.

The third man went behind Jake and placed a Santa's hat on his head.

"Now you fit the role. You could go undercover with this, you know."

They all laughed–except Jake. He snatched the hat off his head and tossed it on top of the box.

"Laugh all you want. Once I'm back, watch out," he snarled.

The others laughed again.

"Hey, Harry did a great job year after year, tough act to follow. Think you can handle it?" the first man asked.

"You know what a kid person Jake is," another one said.

Again the laughter.

"We'll let you get to it."

They turned to leave and caught sight of Shea.

"Whoa, I see you got the best desk in the building, Jake. Leave it to you."

He smiled at Shea. "How're you doing Shea?"

"Same old, same old. What's with the jokes?" she asked.

"Jake's been named this year's Christmas Cop. The guy who arranges the toys for those kids in town who wouldn't have Christmas presents if we didn't pitch in and provide. Perfect for old Jake. He's had it easy the last few weeks. This'll get him used to paperwork for when he gets back on the active duty roster."

The others laughed and waved at her when they left.

Shea looked at Jake. He wasn't laughing.

"You don't look happy about the assignment."

Nothing like stating the obvious.

"What do I know about kids? I'm never around them, heck, I've never even worked juvvie. I don't know what kids want for Christmas. I don't have time to shop for toys, wrap them, decide who gets what and arrange for delivery."

He scowled at the box with the Santa hat on top. "I think my boss hates me."

Shea laughed. "He probably gave the assignment to the best man. How hard can it be?"

"I have no idea. But hard, I bet."

She smiled again, picturing the tough cop buying a princess dolly for a little girl or brightly colored toddler toys.

She hoped he'd embrace the spirit of the season. Christmas was her favorite time. Not only to celebrate the birth of the savior, but to share happiness with others.

It was also the time she missed her family the most.

Weren't cops supposed to serve and protect? So a project to make some kids happy sounded like a great job to her. No worries about someone shooting at him when he delivered presents.

But she could tell from his frown he didn't share her opinion.

She looked back at her code, wondering how Jake would handle his new assignment.

When Shea arrived at her condo after work, she glanced around at the decorations she'd already put up for Christmas. She smiled. She loved coming home to a place ready for the holidays.

Thanksgiving weekend given her the perfect time to get a tree and pull out her ornaments and decorate. She had made a ginger bread house, placed garlands of holly all over, and had three different creches throughout the ground floor. The cinnamon spice fragrance from the ornaments she had made spoke of Christmas, too.

Shrugging off her jacket, she kicked off her shoes and headed for the kitchen. She was hungry, but didn't want to fix a big meal. A sandwich and soup would suit her fine.

As she prepared the meal, she thought about Jake Morgan. He'd been quiet most of the day, even though more and more fellow cops had stopped by to see him through the afternoon. Some seemed genuinely glad to have him back even if only dealing with cold cases.

And a couple teased him about the Christmas assignment.

He'd left before she had. She suspected his ankle was hurting. But he'd probably never admit to that. A macho man in a macho profession.

She couldn't resist smiling at his railing against handling the Christmas for Kids program. He did seem too much of a warrior fighting against evil than Santa.

Shea knew how valuable that program was. How awful it'd be for a child to have a Christmas without decorations or presents. There were other organizations in town that also provided for kids in need. But the Mondano Police Department was the largest at Christmas. She'd heard about it ever since she'd moved here.

Thinking about her own family's Christmas celebrations, she glanced around. She'd done her best to incorporate the special feeling of the season. Yet she knew it'd be even more special at her parents' home. Too bad this year wasn't her year to take off at Christmas.

The firm she and Cal started provided excellent customer service with someone on call all the time—and they meant all the time—even Christmas if a client needed them. Cal handled that holiday last year, this year was her turn.

Once her makeshift meal was ready, she carried it into the living room and turned on the TV. She'd check in later with Cal for any updates, but for now, this time was hers.

Jake popped some ibuprofen as soon as he reached his apartment. Who knew how strenuous sitting at a desk could be? He thought it'd be a piece of cake as his boss liked to say. He felt wiped out.

He grabbed a frozen dinner, zapped it in the microwave and went to the recliner. He might even sleep in it if it saved him moving again, he thought once he was eating. The pills were starting to work and he gradually felt better as he ate.

The cold cases were something he could get into, but that Christmas assignment was something else. He didn't know anything about kids and what they wanted for Christmas. And he'd never organized a project as far reaching as this one.

He donated cash every year to the cause. And left it all to Harry Carmichael. The older man seemed to enjoy it, but Jake didn't know how to even begin.

He was the wrong man for the job.

His boss knew his background. Group home, handouts at Christmas. Sometimes new clothes, sometimes a book or game. He'd never had a train, or action figures, or things boys love.

He shook away the memories. He was grown now, making a life for himself. If he wanted something, he bought it.

Well, except for that sports car. One want he couldn't afford.

Maybe one day.

He figured he'd spend a couple of hours a day on the project and focus the rest of his time on the cold cases. Maybe he'd find a clue that'd break one wide open.

When Jake arrived at work the next morning, Shea was already at her desk, eyes focused on her computer screen.

She glanced up. "Hi."

"Hi," he replied, walking slowly to the desk he'd claimed.

The Christmas project box was on the floor beside his chair. He'd been thinking about it all night it seemed. He'd decided to treat it like another kind of investigation. Lay things out, make a time line chart, and start from that.

When he opened the box he saw a jumble of papers. No order at all.

Shea jumped up and began walking around.

"How long have you been here?" he asked. Usually she went an hour or so between her steps.

"Since six. I spoke with my partner last night and we came up with a different strategy and I was anxious to get started."

She kept walking.

One circuit took her near his desk. She looked into the box.

"What a mess." she said.

"I guess Harry knew where everything was, but it looks like a disaster to me," Jake said.

"Want help sorting it?" she asked.

"Can you afford the time?" He'd be grateful for any help he could get.

"My eyes are going blurry studying the stupid screen. It'll be a change."

He reached in and handed her a stack of papers.

"How shall I sort them?" she asked.

"I have no idea."

He took out another handful and tried to figure out what the sheets represented.

Shea moved to the desk next to his and placed the stack in the middle. Taking up the first page, she skimmed it and put it to the right.

"It looks like these are notes on businesses and stores who contribute each year," she murmured, taking another sheet, and then another.

Jake had the same kinds of information, but the dates weren't consistent. Here was a page from four years ago. Another from six years ago.

"They're not in chronological order," he said in frustration.

Couldn't Harry have had a better process?

"All the more challenging," she said, sorting the papers into three piles.

A few minutes later she came over and took another handful of papers.

"What is the FD he refers to?" she asked at one point.

"I have no idea. I've seen it on some of these pages, too."

Jake checked the box, it was finally empty. He had several stacks of paper on his desk and Shea had several on the one next to his.

"Vendors?"

He took hold of one pile and held it up.

"Yep."

She reached for a pile and picked it up, bringing it over to merge with his.

"Volunteers."

They compiled those pages.

"Something that looks like lists of toys."

"Yep." She handed him that stack.

"Kids."

"I only had a few pages of kids names and they seem old, like from five years ago. That FD is noted next to several," she said. "Did some of this get transferred to the fire department?"

She brought those pages and handed them to Jake.

"Not that I know of."

"It seems to me we should put them in chronological order with the most recent on top. That might be all that's needed to bring organization out of chaos. You could read each year's list to get a good idea of what went on."

"I guess."

He looked at the four stacks and shook his head. He had no idea of what he was doing. And he wanted to get back to that cold case file he'd started reviewing yesterday. He wasn't Santa.

"I'll take these," she said and began putting the names of children pages in some sort of order.

"There're a lot of names on this," she said. "But the list seems to be several years old. Isn't there anything more recent?"

"I have no idea. I'm finding the same thing with the vendors who donate. And that FD noted by a lot of them," he replied.

They continued in silence for several minutes. When finished, Shea sat on the edge of the desk.

"Nothing's more recent than four years. Are you sure these are all the files?"

"As far as I know. I'll ask Janey. She knows everything around here. She's been the division secretary for a decade or more."

"Okay, then."

Shea hopped off the desk and returned to her own. In only minutes she was engrossed in the code.

Jake called Janey.

"Oh, my gosh, Jake, I'm so sorry–I forgot the flash drive. I think Harry used it a lot in the last couple of years. I'll bring it right over."

In less than two minutes Janey rushed into the room with a flash drive held high.

"Here it is. Sorry about that."

"FD–flash drive," Jake said.

Shea swung around and smiled.

"That'll have the up-to-date info I bet. He must have started using that instead of paper."

Jake didn't say anything to Janey, but he was annoyed that the better part of an hour had been spent in sorting papers that he wouldn't need.

He appreciated Shea's help, but knew she must be frustrated at wasting her time.

When Janey left, he put the flash drive into the top drawer.

"Aren't you going to look at it?" Shea asked.

"I've spent enough time on this project this morning. It'll keep until tomorrow."

Shea nodded and resumed her perusal of the code.

"Gotcha!" she yelled a few minutes later.

Jake looked up. "You found the problem?"

"Maybe. It's a problem anyway. We limited some of the sizes of the files we'd compare. I'm not sure who thought that was a good idea–probably me at the time."

"What do you mean who thought it a good idea. Didn't you develop this program?"

"Our company did. We have fifteen programmers on staff. Each did a portion. Including me and Cal. Then we put it together, worked out the bugs and tested it and tested it. But we didn't have actual data, so we made up data to test it."

"Does that mean you're done here?" he asked.

He'd known her for less than two days, but was already used to her hopping up and walking around. And getting used to the occasional conversations they had.

Even the pink hair was growing on him.

He wasn't sure he'd enjoy working alone in the big room.

"Time will tell. This is an easy fix, but it might ripple through the program, so it's back to testing."

"Where's your company located?"

"On Stanton Street, near the warehouse district. The building we have is actually a converted warehouse. Rent's cheap."

"That's where you'll test?"

"If it was still in beta, yes, but this is already installed. Now we'll test here with actual data and your police department IT guys."

She gave him a friendly grin and reached for her cell phone. A moment later she was talking with someone at her company.

Jake looked at the papers in front of him, but couldn't help listening to Shea.

"I found it," Shea told her partner. "At least I hope it's just this one glitch. We limited the size of a data file in the section where we import. So when the date to import was too large, it defaulted to an error. I've fixed it."

"Good job. I knew you'd find it if there was a problem," her partner said. "Do we recompile?"

"Yep. I'll do that overnight. I'll check if they want me to come in tomorrow since it's Saturday. Or wait until Monday. When I do come in, I'll work with the IT department to see if that's it."

"Keep me informed."

"Sure. How are things there?"

"Slow as molasses."

"It is every December. Enjoy."

"Will you be coming into the office any time soon?"

"Don't know. We'll see how this goes. Do you need me for anything?"

"Not really. I haven't seen you in a week. It feels weird without you here. And there are a few programmers who could use your eyes on what they're working on."

"I'll be back soon enough. Have a good weekend. See ya."

3

Jake listened to Shea's side of the conversation. From it he gleaned she'd be staying a bit longer.

But not necessarily in this room. The IT department was on another floor.

As noon approached, Jake looked up as Shea jumped up from her seat and began her walking. Would she offer to pick up lunch again?

"I'm off to Ben's. Do you want anything?" she asked when she'd finished her circuit.

"Same as yesterday, thanks."

"Sure thing."

He reached for his wallet.

"Hey, this one is on me. I'm celebrating finding the glitch. I'll be back soon."

It seemed a long time, but when she returned, the aroma of hamburgers and fries filled the air.

He pushed aside the folder he'd been working on.

Today Shea came over to his desk and began unpacking the food. Then she dragged a chair from a nearby desk, shrugged out of her jacket, and plopped down to eat with him.

"So how did you get into computer programming," he asked.

She was bright and bubbly while the only computer geeks he knew weren't that outgoing.

"I love the order of it. And I like making things happen. I met Cal at college and we clicked. We vowed to start up our own company once we graduated. Which we did. The early days were hard. We moonlighted to make ends meet. But when we sold our first program, we were in the money and put it all back into making the business grow. Now we're doing well, have a bunch of programmers working for us."

She smiled broadly and popped an onion ring into her mouth.

"You don't seem like a geek to me," Jake said.

She laughed. "Good. Keeps others on their toes. You, on the other hand, look just like a cop."

"I do?" he asked, surprised at the comment.

"Yep. Tall, built, with an air of competency and control. And a very stern expression. I bet you're something when you aren't using the cane."

He looked at her closely and saw the teasing in her eyes.

"Are your flirting with me Miss O'Riley?"

"Would you mind if I did?" she asked with a saucy grin.

Then she laughed. "Your expression is priceless. If you're already taken, I'll back off."

He studied her for a moment, taken aback by her line of conversation.

"I'm not seeing anyone right now," he said stiffly.

It'd been months since he'd been on a date. Usually he was caught up in whatever investigation was going on and didn't take time off for dating.

"Me, either."

"What about Cal?"

"What about him? He's my partner. And married to Gwen. They have two adorable twin boys. They're going on vacation at Christmas, leaving me to staff the fort."

"So you're not going anywhere for Christmas?"

"Nope. My folks live in Florida now, so I won't be spending it with them. How about you? Any plans for Christmas?"

He shook his head. "I usually work that week, give guys with families time off."

"Like a lot of tech companies, we close between December 20th and the first working

Monday in January. But we're committed to total customer service, so Cal and I trade off holidays to be available. This is my be-available-at-Christmas-year. With any luck no one will be working and having problems so I'll have nothing to do. So what about this year?"

"What do you mean? You just said it was your year."

"You. You can't work your normal job so what are your plans this year?"

He shrugged and finished his burger. "No plans."

She leaned closer. "Want to spend the day with me? It's a lonely day if I'm by myself and don't have an emergency to go out on. Of course there's always that possibility. You'd have to be prepared for that. What about it?"

No one had asked Jake to spend Christmas with them before—except his partner.

He'd felt like an outsider at their home that first year. In-laws, aunts and uncles, cousins and Phil's own family crowded his home. Even though Phil asked every year, Jake had stopped accepting the invitations.

"Doing?" he asked.

"Celebrating, of course. I can come pick you up and take you home if you can't drive. I'll have a ham and all the fixings–and plum pudding of course. It's my mama's recipe and it'll knock your socks off it's so good."

He hesitated a moment, then shrugged. "Okay."

"Wow, don't blow me away with your enthusiasm," she teased.

He studied her as they ate. She was like a ray of sunshine. Her optimism reigned. She was persuasive without being obvious about it.

He couldn't believe he'd accepted her invitation for Christmas Day.

"So you know, I can drive. It's my left ankle that's broken, not my right one."

"Okay then. Come around ten on Christmas morning."

He nodded. That was still three weeks away. Would they get to know each other better in that time? Or would she be gone once the program fix was approved by the IT guys?

She finished her onion rings, swiped one of his fries and balled up the wrapping paper.

"I'm done for the day. I'll recompile the program overnight and be ready to test first thing Monday. I told Captain Robbins I need to talk to him this afternoon to make sure waiting over the weekend is okay with him. Until he can see me,

I'm free. Want any help with the Christmas Cop thing?"

He frowned. "I'm in the middle of a file on a cold case. I'd rather continue on that."

"Okay. Then I'll see you Monday."

In only moments she was gone.

Jake looked at her desk, already missing her. He frowned. He didn't miss people.

She didn't disturb him when he was focused on the case. He hardly knew she was there. Unless he counted her walking around the room every hour.

Now he'd miss it.

"Get used to it, dude," he murmured. "If she found the glitch, she'll be gone for good."

Would she even remember the Christmas invitation in three weeks?

For the first time in years, Jake hoped he'd be spending Christmas with someone.

Shea went to update Captain Robbins on the situation, then wandered to the IT section for the police department. It was comprised of three men and a woman who handled all the computer requests.

"Hi guys," she said as she breezed into their small work room. It was cooler here than the rest of the building. She wished she'd put on a sweater.

"Hey, Shea. Find the glitch yet?" Stan asked.

"I think so. One anyway. I'll recompile it and then we can try it out. Are you planning to work tomorrow?"

"Most of us have the weekend off. Brian will be here, but we can wait for Monday. He's here to handle emergencies, not the routine work on the weekends. What was the problem?"

Knowing they'd understand–unlike Captain Robbins who had brushed aside the details, only wanting to know it'd work–she explained the code she believed was limiting the program. The five of them discussed the ramifications and agreed to test it out together Monday morning.

Once they finished with their discussion, Shea took off for her office. She'd see if there was anything crucial needing her attention there. Working off site had its limits.

Jake closed the file. Nothing out of the ordinary. No clues that hadn't been followed. No definitive suspects. While still technically an open case, he had nothing to offer that would lead to the murderer.

He rubbed his eyes and glanced at his watch. He could head for home. No one would begrudge him a couple of hours.

He was annoyed at himself for feeling tired after sitting at a desk all day. He needed to get back in shape if he was going to pass the physical to resume full time duty. He wondered if the gym had any programs for those who couldn't use their leg?

He opened the top drawer and took out the flash drive. Might as well do some recon on this to see what he was up against. He put it in the computer and double clicked. In a moment he had the list of files displayed.

Kids. Vendors. Volunteers. Organizations. The latter probably companies that participated with direct financial donations.

He doubled clicked on vendors. Gibberish filled the screen. Jake frowned. Wasn't this a self operating program? Did he need to open it in some other program? He exited out of the drive and pulled it out. He wasn't going to deal with this today.

Though he'd have to get started soon. Christmas was approaching faster than he liked.

He resented he'd been given the assignment, but that didn't mean he didn't plan to do a good job.

He'd deal with it Monday morning. He'd relish the weekend to catch up on rest and be in better form come Monday.

Shea headed for her home-away-from-home-office early Monday morning to dump her stuff on her desk. Then she'd head for IT. She wanted to see Jake before getting down to work.

Mainly for the Christmas assignment, she told herself. But she knew that wasn't the only reason. Maybe not even the most important reason.

She'd thought about him a lot over the weekend. He intrigued her.

He was good looking yet didn't seem to play off that like some men did. He was reticent about his own life, didn't gossip like some liked to do or flirt.

If he ever smiled, she'd missed it.

She couldn't help smiling herself remembering his reaction to being the Christmas Cop. Despite that, she suspected he'd give it his all. He didn't seem like a man who would slough off any responsibility given him.

Sipping her coffee, she sat at her desk and turned on the computer. The program had recompiled over the weekend. Now she wanted Stan to try what he'd done before that brought up the glitch. She hoped this was the only problem. She didn't want the PD to think her company wasn't up to designing the custom program they'd asked for.

She heard the thumps and smiled, watching the doorway.

A moment later he stepped into the room, surprised to see her evident in his expression.

"Did you do the testing already?" he asked, walking over to his desk.

"Not yet. I'm waiting for Stan to call to say he's ready. They have other work to do, so I'm in a waiting mode right now."

"Maybe you can help me out," Jake said, shrugging off his jacket, sitting down and turning on his computer.

"Sure, with what?"

"I tried the flash drive before I left Friday, but couldn't get it opened right. Maybe it's using a program I don't have."

He retrieved it from the desk and plugged into his computer.

Shea took a last swallow of her coffee, tossed the cup into the trash, and went to his desk.

"Show me," she said leaning over his shoulder.

Jake caught the sweet scent she was wearing and for a moment forgot what he was doing.

From the corner of his eye he could see her pink hair. It looked as soft and fluffy as cotton candy. Was it silky to the touch? Or had the dye made it coarse?

"So go to that drive and double click," she instructed.

Did she think he didn't know that much? He quickly tried to open the vendor file.

The same gibberish filled the screen.

"It's a standard excel file," she said, leaning over to reach the key board, brushing against his shoulder as she did.

"Hmmm," she said using the mouse to move the cursor.

A click and she was back to the list of files.

She studied them a moment and then reached over his shoulder again to use the mouse and made the description column larger.

Jake kept his face forward, his eyes on the computer screen. But he was tempted to turn slightly to the right. Her face was inches from his.

He could feel the warmth from her body.

She pulled up the excel software and tried opening the file labeled kids.

Same result.

She tried the others without any better success.

"This drive looks to be corrupted," she said, standing up and moving around the desk so he could see her.

"Which means?"

He was relieved she'd moved away. Being so close had been too tempting.

"Who knows? There're several ways data can get corrupted. I don't suppose there's a back up?"

"I'll check."

After speaking with Janey, Jake hung up shaking his head. "No, this is all she had."

"And the paper files we sorted yesterday aren't current."

"I'm screwed, aren't I?" he asked.

"Let me look at the drive. I might be able to pull some of the data from it."

"Worse case I can call for the vendors' updates using the paper files. I could even check with volunteers if they're still willing to help. But I need those kids names. The paper list is too old.

Without them, I have no idea who needs gifts."

"Gotcha. I'll work on that one first," Shea said.

Shea's phone rang.

"Rats. It's IT. I'll have to do that before I can look at the flash drive."

"It's not your problem anyway."

He was disappointed she was already leaving. He knew this wasn't her problem. The project was his. She was here for a different reason. There was nothing to say she had to help at all.

"Maybe not, but if I can help, why not? See you in a bit."

It was after one when Shea returned.

"Want lunch?" she asked heading for her desk. "I'm starving."

"Let me treat this time," Jake said, fishing money from his wallet.

"Okay. Same as always?"

He almost smiled. Always was three days. If he didn't count the weekend. Yet he liked the sound of it.

"Yeah. Why change a good thing?"

"We should eat better," she commented picking up his money. "And I usually do, but Ben's is temporary for me, so I'm indulging."

"Cops aren't known for nutritious eating," he said.

"I haven't seen you eat a single donut in all the time I've known you."

He smiled at that. "Like you've known me a long time.

4

Shea stopped for a moment, then turned to continue out the door.

Wow, that smile was totally unexpected. It made her feel warm and bubbly. When he smiled he didn't look like a mean cop out to save the world. He looked–sexy.

Whoa, where did that come from?

Shea wasn't one to deny facts. She liked him.

She felt some pull of attraction when she was around him. And if she thought he was sexy when he smiled at her like that she wasn't going to deny it.

But wow again. If he smiled more often, he'd have to beat women off with a stick.

So maybe it was a good thing he didn't.

Except for her.

She wondered what she could do to make him smile more often.

The sooner she picked up their lunch, the sooner she'd be back to share it with Jake.

When she returned and they had opened the wrappers on their lunches, Shea asked him why he'd become a cop. She was interested in learning more about him.

Jake thought about it a moment.

"It seemed like the thing to do at the time. I went to junior college and took some courses in criminology. Sounded like something I could get involved with. I like the forensic aspects and the psychology of the criminal mind. I also like the feeling of belonging to an organization that does good."

"How did you get hurt? Did you get shot?"

He shook his head. "No, I was chasing a guy and had to jump a fence. When I landed wrong in a pile of trash my ankle just snapped."

"And the other guy?"

"Phil came around the other way and caught him."

"Phil?"

"My partner. He's been in a couple of times. He brought the Santa hat."

She laughed. "Okay, I remember him."

"Yeah. There'll be payback."

She laughed again.

Then looking at him, she asked, "Don't your parents worry about you getting shot?"

She knew from their previous discussion they didn't live nearby or he wouldn't be spending Christmas alone.

"No parents. They died when I was really little."

"Oh, sorry about that."

She became silent, focused on eating lunch.

"It was a long time ago. I don't even remember them," he said softly.

She looked at him. "That's sad."

He shrugged. "It is what it is."

"So did grandparents raise you?" she asked.

"No. I grew up in a group home. Worked my way through the two years I went to college and then got on with the police department."

"And now you're a detective, right?"

He nodded.

"There's not a whole lot of crime in Mondano is there?"

She always felt it was a safe place to be.

"You'd be surprised. Not as much as LA or Chicago, but enough to keep the police force at its current staffing level. Without enough staff to continue on the cold cases unless it's someone like me, on the DL."

She ate in silence for a moment.

"You probably have parents, siblings,

grandparents, aunts and uncles and who knows how many best friends" he said.

She nodded with a grin. "Yep. Only one grandfather has passed, the rest live in Indiana, where I'm from. Except for my parents who are in Florida and my brother in Chicago. Everyone thought they were crazy to move to Florida, but Dad said he was tired of the snow every winter, so off they went when my brother got out of school. Their place is nice, right on a lake. But mosquitoes are horrible in summer and the humidity is more than I'd like to live with long term."

"Lucky you."

"I guess that's why the lieutenant assigned you as Christmas Cop," she said a moment later.

"Why?"

"You'd know the importance of making Christmas special for kids who might not get it otherwise. I think it's a great program and I want to help this year. I'm practically a part of the department."

She met his gaze with her sparkling eyes.

"Hardly. But if you want to help, I'm all for it," he said.

"Help only. Don't think you can push it off to me. I think it's important that kids see men in action doing good things. You know most kids are raised by women until they're in high school. Think about it—mothers, school teachers, Sunday school teachers, social workers if needed, almost always women. Both boys and girls need strong male role models."

"I don't see myself as a role model," Jake said, struck by the idea.

"Doesn't mean you aren't."

She gathered the trash and tossed it.

"Let me have the flash drive."

When he gave it to her, she went to her computer and began to work on the task.

A short time later, she looked up.

"I think I can recover most of the data. There'll be gaps, but it'll give us a good start."

When she printed out the database a little later, it was five pages long.

Jake looked up from the file he was studying and took the pages she handed him.

"As far as I can tell, this is the updated kids list from last year," she said. "Some have addresses, most have the ages as of last year, so I guess we add a year. Some have phone numbers."

"There must be a hundred kids here," Jake said.

The size of the task just quadrupled in his mind.

"I'll work on the volunteer list next, so we can get some help from people who know how it worked last year."

"Thanks."

"No problem."

The afternoon began as others had, with Shea working on her computer, jumping up periodically to walk around the room, then resuming her place at the monitor.

Only now Jake knew she was working on the lists of vendors, volunteers and kids, and not some program that didn't work.

Mid afternoon Janey came in accompanied by a young boy. Shea looked up taking in the too small jacket that didn't even zip shut and the worn shoes.

"Jake, this is Jason Billingsley. He wants to talk to the Christmas cop," she said with a smile at the boy. "This is Jake Morgan, the man in charge this year."

The boy looked half scared as he took in Jake's frowning demeanor.

Shea glared at Jake. She wanted to tell him to lighten up, the boy wasn't a crook, and was probably scared to be here in the first place.

Jason stepped bravely into the room. Janey gave him a pat on the shoulder and left.

"What can I do for you?" Jake asked, leaning back in his chair.

"You give the toys for Christmas?" the boy asked.

"Yes."

"I want you to make sure you give Susie Taylor a special doll. She's five and has never had a doll. She's in kindergarten and she can play with toys there, but she can't take them home."

Jake nodded. "What special doll?"

The boy reached in his pocket and pulled out a tattered sheet of paper.

"This one," he said, looking at the catalog page.

Shea watched the exchange. The kid was probably too scared of Jake to step closer, but she knew he couldn't see the doll from his desk.

"Which doll," she asked, rising to walk over to the boy.

He looked at her in surprise his eyes wide.

The pink hair, she knew.

He held out the paper. It showed a doll that opened and closed her eyes and even came with a layette set.

"She is special," Shea said, taking the paper. "Where does Susie live?"

"In my apartment building. She's three doors down," he replied, seeming more comfortable as the minutes ticked by.

"And that is where?"

"I can't tell you," he said. "My mom said don't tell strangers where I live or my name or anything."

"Your mom's absolutely right. But you can tell a police officer, can't you?" Shea asked.

He nodded.

Shea glanced over at Jake.

"He's a cop, but you better ask for identification before you tell him."

She grinned.

Jake gave her a look and reached in his pocket and pulled out his badge, flashing it at the kid.

"I live at 3762 Belvia Street, apartment 17," Jason recited.

"Got it," Jake said, jotting it down. "We'll see what we can do," he said looking at Jason. "Thanks for coming in."

Jason nodded and turned to leave.

"How did you get here?" Jake asked.

The boy looked back, a scared expression on his face.

"I took the bus. I have a student card, so the bus is free."

"Hold on a minute and I'll see if I can get you a ride home. Belvia's quite a ways from here."

Jason looked at Shea and then back to Jake but didn't say anything.

Jake made a call, arranged things, and then hung up.

"I have a police officer ready to take you home in a squad car," he said. "Would you like that?"

Jason's eyes grew huge and his smile matched.

"That would be so cool!"

"If you're real nice to the cop, he might let you sound the siren," Jake added.

Shea smiled at the delight on the boy's face.

A moment later a uniformed police officer entered. "You Jason?"

"Yes, sir."

"I'm Bob Tucker, want to take a ride?"

"Yes, sir."

Bob nodded at Jake, flashed a smile at Shea and led the boy out.

"Who knew you'd be a sucker for a kid," Shea said turning back to her desk. "Maybe you're the right man for the Christmas job after all."

"Belvia Street isn't in the best neighborhood in

the city. Plus seeing him reminded me of me when I was a kid. That jacket needs to be replaced."

"And you'd have loved to ride in a police cruiser when you were that age, I bet."

He nodded.

"A small enough gesture to give him something he'll probably always remember."

Shea nodded, her opinion of the man growing.

He might put on a tough front, but she suspected the more he delved into this project, the more he'd be caught up in it.

As the afternoon wound down, Shea closed up her computer. She'd deal with the rest in the morning.

"I'm off, I'll be here in the morning and finish salvaging what I can from the other corrupted files."

Jake nodded, planning to head out himself soon.

Shea had just begun to pick up where she left off in capturing what she could of the volunteer list the next morning when her phone rang. She saw it was the IT guys upstairs.

"I'm off," she said. "Not sure when I'll be back."

The test run Stan tried worked. The IT group had begun entering actual data the previous day and found the program worked perfectly–allowing for the different parameters of some of the data, depending on how old the input was.

Shea spent most of the morning making sure everything went the way it was designed to work. They tried all the different features to make sure things were working. Shea grew more and more confident as the morning progressed. Nothing glitched.

She went back downstairs when it was lunch time.

Jake was leaning back in his chair, gazing at the ceiling.

She looked up but saw nothing out of the ordinary.

"So, what's up?" she asked.

"Just thinking. I might have to go to the evidence locker later. There's a piece of evidence I want to examine for this case."

"Lunch in the meantime?" she asked.

He nodded and pulled out his wallet.

Shea took his money and left to get their food. She looked forward to lunch each day since Jake arrived. She loved talking with him, learning more about the man, and was pleased to see he seemed as curious about her as she was about him.

Though she wasn't sure he meant to be funny, she laughed at some of the stories he told. He had a dry sense of humor, so maybe he was leading her on after all.

Once lunch was finished, she offered to call some of the volunteers. She wanted to hang out at the police station in case any other problem arose with the new program. This way she'd help out and still be available if needed in IT.

"I'm heading to evidence," he said.

She listened until the thump of the walking cast could no longer be heard, then dialed the first number on the list. Her time here was growing short. Unless she could come up with some reason to stay, tomorrow she'd be back at her own office.

Though, when she thought about it, there was nothing pressing at the office. She could stay longer if she wanted.

If Cal needed her, she'd have to go. But for the time being, she'd stay to help with the Christmas project.

5

Shea dialed the first name on the volunteer list. After explaining who she was and why she was calling, she received a wealth of information from Betsy Samson, one of the volunteers who had volunteered at Christmas for several years.

When she finished the call, she started a time line for all the things that needed to be done—from contacting vendors who provided clothing or toys, to verifying names, ages, sizes and addresses of the kids, to rallying the volunteers for wrapping packages and the cops for distribution.

They needed to contact St. Anne's to see if they could hold the wrapping party there as in previous years. If so they'd stage the presents there as they came in for volunteers to wrap.

And there was a special list of those who needed food supplies as well as other necessities.

While the size of the project seemed huge, Shea refused to let herself become overwhelmed. They could do this.

The police department could do this. They'd handled it for years. She just hadn't had an inkling of how complex it was before.

She liked challenges.

Would Jake see it the same way?

She called Cal.

"Hey, what's up?" he answered.

"I'm going to be tied up here a bit longer."

He groaned. "Now what?"

"I sort of got involved with the project the police do each year in giving toys to kids in need at Christmas."

"Sort of? Like you jumped right in and now are knee deep?" he said giving a chuckle. "I know you, Shea. Couldn't someone else do it?"

"Maybe, but I want to. Things are quiet, you said so earlier. So unless something pops up, I'm going to stay here and see it through."

"Okay. If something comes up I'll holler, but otherwise, I'll know to find you still at the cop shop."

"We might need a bit more help," she said slowly.

"As in?"

She explained the situation, ending with, "So according to the volunteer, all that group does is wrap presents and stage for delivery. Then on the day before Christmas Eve it's all hands on deck to deliver them. Any chance you or the gang would help? The more the merrier."

"Help in what exactly," he asked cautiously.

"First in compiling the data needed to know what to get each child. There's a list, but the flash drive it's on is corrupted and I don't think I have all the data. So it'll mean calling around to fill in the blanks. Then we need to keep an accurate spreadsheet of age, sizes, toys wanted, that kind of thing."

"All on a volunteer basis, I'm sure," Cal said.

"Of course."

"Anyplace to work there or will we be doing it from here?"

"There's really limited space here. But a lot can be done from our office. See who wants to help."

"Will do. Anything else, like how's the program going now?"

"Oops, I should have started with that. It seems to be working fine and they're using it with real data with no problems."

"That's good to hear," he said. "I'll call you back when I see who wants in."

"Thanks, Cal. This is going to be a great way to get ready for Christmas."

"Humph," he replied before saying goodbye.

Shea grinned at his response. He was a softy at heart.

She suspected he'd present it to the staff as a super opportunity to give back at Christmas and everyone would be on board.

She updated the list of children as best she could from the corrupted data. Once she had a spreadsheet to her satisfaction, she emailed it to Cal with full confidence members of their team would rally around and start calling to fill in the blanks.

Turning to the volunteer file, she worked on getting as much data from that one as she could. She'd make a few calls to see who was available this year and what they could do. And asked each one if they knew anyone else who might want to be involved.

Shea was so engrossed in her task she didn't notice the tell-tale thump along the hall and was startled when Jake appeared in the doorway.

"What, you couldn't hear me a mile away," he said noting her surprise.

She shook her head. "Guess not. Any luck in finding the killer?"

"A promising lead actually. A couple of things to check on first, but I definitely suspect someone.

Any luck with the volunteers?"

"I've only talked to a couple. So far what I'm discovering is they wrap presents and sort them by child. Some even deliver to help out. They haven't been involved in collecting the items. That, apparently, was Harry's part."

Jake sat in his chair and frowned.

"I know nothing about buying things for kids."

She picked up a printed copy of one of her spreadsheets and carried it over to him.

"I hope I haven't overstepped my bounds, but I've got this under control."

She put it in front of him.

"Names, ages, addresses, wants, needs and sizes," he read the headings.

"I've got people calling to get updated information. Once we have a complete list, we can sort by each heading if we need to."

"So?"

"So if kids need new jackets, we can sort by needs, then sizes, then order that many."

He nodded. "Toys?"

"With this many kids, I'm sure there're going to be some duplicates in the toy department, same thing. We order however many of what kind we want. The complicated part comes in wrapping and labeling and sorting so each family's complete," she said, skimming over the top sheet.

Jake studied the pages.

"We'll want to put them all together once wrapped so each volunteer takes all the presents to each family and we don't have them crossing each other in the driveway," Shea continued.

He looked at it again, flipped up a couple of pages.

"Lots of names," he said.

"One hundred fifteen to be precise," she said. "And that's before anyone else might show up like Jason did to ask for someone else to be included."

"Is he on here?"

She nodded. "And I added Susie, too. We should find out about the other kids in her family if there are any."

Jake looked at her. "You should be running this. You've got it covered."

She smiled and shook her head.

"This is a Mondano PD event. I'll help, but you're the Christmas Cop."

He scowled again.

Shea laughed.

"I've got a list of places to call to see if they can collect the presents and hold until Christmas Eve, but I think it'll be more likely to be offered if you make the calls."

She gave him a list and updated him on what the volunteers told her.

He glanced at the folder he'd carried up from Evidence, clearly wanting to get back to his cold case. Glancing at his watch, he nodded and picked up the phone to start making calls.

Shea was ready to call it a day. She'd visited the IT department again, pleased to see everything was progressing smoothly. Fingers crossed that one little correction was all the new program needed to work flawlessly.

Stan and the others were pleased with their accomplishments getting closer to catching up to where they'd hoped to be by now.

She shut down her computer.

Jake looked up. "Leaving?"

"Yes. It's been a long day."

"Want to have dinner together?" he asked.

Shea looked at him, surprised by the invitation. "Tonight?"

"Do you like Chinese?" he asked, nodding his head.

"Sure."

"There's a place a few blocks over."

"Okay. Now?"

"If you can hold on a few minutes, I'll wrap up here and we can leave. It'll be an early dinner, but we'll beat any crowd."

She nodded and sat down, uncertain by this turn of events.

Probably he wanted to talk more about the Christmas project. She had a skill for organization, from organizing computer code to be most efficient, she thought. She hoped she'd covered everything.

Shea met Jake at the restaurant. While only a few blocks away, she knew that'd be too far for him to walk with his broken ankle. But she relished the exercise. It was cold, but dry. The air felt invigorating.

As it turned out, there was limited parking by the restaurant, so she was glad she'd walked.

Stepping inside, Shea's mouth began watering.

"It smells divine in here," she said with a happy smile at him.

She loved all kinds of food, and hadn't had Chinese in a while, so this was a treat.

They were seated in a booth near the front.

Once they ordered plates to share, Shea looked at Jake.

"Did you want to talk about the Christmas project?"

He shook his head.

"Not especially. It looks like more work than I expected, but thinking on it, Harry was pretty much off the duty roster each December. I should have expected it to be more than a quick fix. But we can talk about it at work."

"So why the dinner invitation?"

His gaze seemed uncertain. He cleared his throat. A sign of nervousness?

Not possible, Shea thought.

"I wanted to see you, that's all. Away from work."

"Oh."

A warm glow settled near her heart.

She found him fascinating. Did he have a similar interest in her? That would be way cool.

He continued to look at her and Shea floundered around for something to talk about.

It'd be totally awkward if they just sat here silently staring at each other.

"So, have you decorated your place for Christmas yet?" she asked brightly.

He shook his head.

"I'm not much for decorations. For the most part, it's just another day for me. I usually work as I told you."

She remembered he had no family to celebrate with. And that she'd invited him to spend the day with her.

It'd been an off the cuff invitation, but she

really hoped he'd follow through on his acceptance.

"Let me guess, you have," he said.

She smiled. "You bet. The minute Thanksgiving was over, it was time to get ready for Christmas. I did my shopping early for my parents since I needed to ship their presents to Florida. I love this holiday and enjoy decorating so I feel the joyful spirit every time I go home."

"What besides a tree?"

"Holly garlands, pine cones, candy canes and little decorations all around. And, of course, a creche to celebrate the baby Jesus' birth."

He nodded.

When the meal was served, the talk gradually moved to where they lived and then what they did for recreation. Shea wasn't surprised to find he was more of a workaholic than someone who relished down time.

Similar to her.

She found computer work fascinating and never seemed to get tired of it.

She asked him more about the circumstances around his injured ankle and the conversation veered in another direction. His frustration at being limited came through in his recounting the weeks at home when he could do very little.

"So even desk duty is better than hanging out at my place," he finished.

"And it'll be all the better if you end up solving one of the cold cases."

He nodded. "I won't feel like it's merely busy work if that happens."

When they finished, Jake learned she'd walked to the restaurant. He offered to drop her back at the police station to pick up her own car.

"I'm good with a walk. And it's only a few blocks. Who'd be out wanting to mug anyone as cold as it is tonight," she said as she walked with him to his car.

"Thank you for a fun evening and good food," she said, smiling up at him before he opened his car door.

"I enjoyed it, too."

He hesitated only a second before leaning over and kissing her lightly.

Shea felt heat rocket through her.

When he pulled back she felt abandoned. She wanted to grab him and go for another kiss.

But he gave a half smile and said good night.

Almost in a daze she watched as he got into his car and started the engine.

She waved as he pulled away, then turned to walk back to her car. Or float back, almost.

A totally unexpected evening.

Shea spent a restless night reliving the kiss and wondering if it meant anything, or was just a way to end a pleasant evening.

She didn't want to read anything into it that wasn't there.

But she was more than willing to imagine a future that included lots more kisses from her solemn cop.

6

The next morning, Shea decided to postpone seeing Jake. She'd spent a restless night and felt unsure of her own emotions.

She decided to head for her office. She'd stopped by several times during her sojourn at the police department, but still there were piles of mail, non-urgent phone messages, and a stack of updates on various projects their company had contracted all sitting on her desk.

Might as well get through as much as she could this morning.

Cal arrived shortly after she'd plunged into reviewing all the current projects, trying to get a handle on things that'd happened while she'd been focused on the glitch in the police program.

"Hey stranger. I didn't know you'd be in today," he greeted her, holding his cup of coffee.

Shea smiled as she returned the greeting.

He always had a cup of coffee in hand until noon. Once the magic hour arrived, he didn't drink any more until the next morning. She guessed he went through about six cups before noon every day.

"Thought I'd better make an appearance before the rest of you forgot me," she said with a grin.

"Like that'd ever happen. Are you satisfied the PD program is fine?"

"I hovered over them a few times yesterday to see if anything cropped up, but it seems to be going great. They know to call if anything else comes up, but so far so good. I think it was just that one glitch, so they should be good for years ahead. I'm looking over some of the other project updates. Martin seems about ready for beta with the program he's working on."

"I know, cool, huh? Super fast, so I'm a bit leery the beta test will be flawless, but he's a genius, so it could be good from the get go."

"Did you ask everyone about helping with the kids?"

"Yep, and everyone's on board. In fact we started yesterday calling from that list you sent. I made an executive decision to allocate the hours between four and six for calls. No trying to do it haphazardly."

"An executive decision, huh?" she said with a smile.

They normally made decisions together, but she was pleased he was so on board.

Cal shrugged, took another sip of coffee. "You back for good now?"

"I don't know. I might spend some time at the cop shop working on the Christmas project. I know most of that I can do here. Maybe."

"Great, that's definitive. Go if you need to, but don't forget this is where you really belong."

"Never. Now go on and let me get back to work or I'll feel like I'm starting over."

He nodded and moved on to his office.

Shea was well into reviewing the updates when her phone rang.

"O'Riley," she answered.

"Where are you?" Jake asked.

"At work. Where are you?"

"At work and I'm not seeing you. Are you up in IT?"

"No, actually I'm at my work, catching up. The Mondano PD isn't our only client, you know."

He was silent for a moment.

"Fair enough. Are you coming here today?"

She thought about their kiss. Would things be

awkward between them?

Or was she the only one even thinking about it?

"Do you need me to come in? There isn't much I could do there that I can't do here. And we're in a holding pattern anyway until all the kids' parents have been contacted. Until then we don't know what to ask for in donations or what to tell volunteers about wrapping the presents and delivery. Did you get a place for us to store the presents?"

"St. Anne's will do it again. It's Harry's home church, they've done it for years and are welcoming us again—even with Harry out of the game."

"Good. So, anything else?"

"No."

There was silence on the line for a moment.

Shea was about to say goodbye when he spoke again.

"The kiss isn't freaking you out, is it?"

"It was unexpected," she said slowly.

"Unwelcomed? If so it won't happen again," he replied.

"Oh no, not unwelcomed."

She made a face. That was too quick.

"I mean, it was nice."

Jake chuckled. "Great, men like to hear things like that. Nice. It's a wimpy word."

"So you'd prefer something like it knocked my socks off and wow, where did you learn to kiss like that and how soon can you do it again?"

He laughed outright. "Yeah, that'd work."

"It was nice," she repeated, smiling broadly.

Some of the previous statement was true, but she wasn't telling him that.

"I'll try to do better next time," he said softly.

Shea's heart beat skyrocketed.

"Okay then, we'll see."

"So are you coming in today or not?"

"Not. I've got lots to do here."

"So when?"

"I'll keep you updated by phone," she stalled.

She didn't want him to think she was skittish after that kiss, but she was. She wasn't exactly sure how she felt.

"Right. Talk to you soon, then."

She slowly put her phone down on the desk.

She was a chicken, no doubt about it. Jake had sounded confident and sure of himself.

She should be, too. She'd dated. She'd kissed a lot of men.

But none had touched her like his kiss last night.

Shaking her head, she tried to get back into review mode and get caught up on her company's projects.

Shea brought home Mexican take out at the end of the day. She looked forward to a night of vegging out, eating a favorite meal and maybe even going to bed early.

There was nothing on television she wanted to see, so she picked up a mystery book she'd bought a couple of weeks ago but hadn't started. Reading as she ate, she was soon engrossed in trying to follow the clues.

When a knock sounded, she reluctantly put aside the book and headed for the door.

Opening it, she was surprised to see Jake standing there.

"I didn't expect to see you," Shea said, gesturing for him to come inside the apartment.

"Hope I'm not intruding," he said, stepping in, and looking around, taking in all the Christmas decorations displayed.

"Wow, you must love Christmas."

"I do."

She closed the door and glanced at the messy dining table. If she'd known she'd have company she'd have cleaned up as soon as she finished eating.

What was he doing here?

"Have a seat," she said.

He shrugged out of his heavy jacket and tossed it across a chair. Moving to the front of the sofa, he sat.

Shea noticed the folder in his hand. She quickly went to sit on the coffee table near him, their knees almost touching.

"Something come up with the project?" she asked.

"I spent more time today than I wanted trying to line up vendors. They all ask questions about the items wanted, quantity, where to deliver, dates. Nothing I couldn't handle, except I need the feedback your team's getting to answer specifics."

"I didn't even check with them today, too busy with other things," Shea said slowly.

She should have jumped right on that to make sure her employees help could be utilized but was distracted catching up on everything that had happened while she was working at police headquarters.

"I'll check first thing tomorrow," she promised.

"Will you go with me to some of the stores in town? I want to see what I'm ordering, to have a better idea of what we'll have. Sorting and distributing's going to be a nightmare, I think."

"If we know who gets what, when we're wrapping presents, we can sort and label. You need to make sure the volunteers know how to do that, but it should go smoothly if we identify everything for each child."

"I spoke with the priest at St. Anne's and he suggested December 21st as wrapping day. Close enough to delivery date, but maybe it won't interfere with plans volunteers might have closer to Christmas itself. Plus he has a group at the church who want to help wrap as well."

"Good. So we have to have everything there by that morning. I doubt there'll be a problem. What's in the folder?"

"Volunteers. I called a few today, but mostly reached answering machines. So far no one's called back. I also got a sign-up going at the station."

He ran his fingers through his hair.

"And so far I've spent more time on this than the cold case I'm working on."

"But those'll be there after Christmas. You have a hard deadline for this."

"True. I'm a cop, I'm used to looking at clues, weighing evidence, not corralling people for a service project. I'm not even sure how to plan for the wrapping night."

"Think of it logistically. Have you seen the space at St. Anne's?"

He shook his head.

Shea thought a minute, then rose and went to get a tablet.

"Okay, we'll make a list. First check out the space at the church so we'll know how large it is. Can we put toys in one area and tables for wrapping in another, and a place for finished presents with labels?"

She looked at him, then jotted the questions on her tablet.

"Someone needs to pull the toys or clothes according to the master list and give them to a volunteer to wrap, keeping them all together."

She nodded and added that to the list she was compiling.

"Then put all the wrapped presents in the order we'll be distributing."

"We need to know where the volunteers are going and also stage presents by neighborhoods so we don't have people going back and forth all over town."

"What a nightmare," Jake said, running his fingers through his hair again.

"Naw, we'll have everything on the spreadsheet, sort it by location, then by family, then by kid. It'll be a piece of cake."

"Yeah, my lieutenant says that when some tricky arrest is eminent."

Shea laughed softly.

"This'll work, I guarantee it. You'll be renowned for your handling of this project. They'll probably ask you next year, too."

"No! This is only because I'm on the disabled list."

"We'll see," she murmured, adding some notes to her list.

She knew he felt out of his depth with this project, but she knew he was doing all the right things. It was all for kids, after all.

She liked seeing him involved so intently. He may think he was wrong for the assignment, but she knew he was perfect.

Jake leaned back and looked around.

"Where do you store all this when it's not the Christmas season?" he asked, taking in the displays of little houses with lights shining inside, the skating scene, the ornaments and greenery.

"Well the tree and garlands go in the trash at the end. The other things pack up in only five boxes, which I keep in the storage area in my garage."

"And how long did it take you to decorate this place?"

"Most of Black Friday. I don't want to fight the crowds, so my tradition is to set up for Christmas that day."

"Are you coming to the station tomorrow?" he asked.

"Do I need to?"

He nodded, watching her closely.

"Why?"

"It's easier to work together if we're in the same room," he said.

"As opposed to phone calls?" she asked.

Did she want to go back to the police headquarters? She was trying not to read anything into a friendly kiss.

But she did miss being there, eating lunch together, bouncing ideas off each other.

"You're the techie, I prefer face to face," he replied.

"Okay, I'll come in tomorrow morning. Then we'll see if I need to stay all day."

He nodded.

Shea waited for him to say something else, but he remained silent, looking around at the decorations.

"So, what now?" she asked after several minutes of silence.

"Want to call volunteers?" he asked meeting her gaze.

"Not particularly. I take it you have no plans for tonight."

He shook his head.

"Want to watch a Christmas movie?" she asked.

"Which one," he asked suspiciously.

Shea laughed. "What's your favorite? I have a streaming service, I bet most Christmas movies are available from now to Christmas."

"I don't have a favorite. I'm not sure I've even watched a Christmas movie before," he said slowly.

"Ah, then we'll watch *It's a Wonderful Life*. It's one of my favorites and if you haven't seen it, you'll be in for a treat."

She jumped up and went into the open kitchen, still able to see him.

"Want some popcorn? I love to watch movies with popcorn."

"Sure."

Shea was glad to have something to do rather than being so close to Jake she longed to reach out and touch him.

To ask more about how his day had gone.

To learn more about him.

It didn't take long for the popcorn to pop. She dumped it into a large bowl.

"Soda to drink okay?"

"Yeah, I'll take a cola."

She took two cans from the refrigerator and headed back to the living room with the popcorn.

She didn't hesitate to sit beside him. The sofa offered the best view of her television. Placing the bowl between them, drinks on the coffee table, she smiled at Jake.

"Feel free to put your feet up if you want. To me, that's the purpose of a coffee table."

In only moments, she'd found the movie and started it playing.

She felt when Jake relaxed. He leaned back, engrossed in the movie, taking some popcorn from time to time. When he opened his soda can, he also opened hers. Before the movie was twenty minutes along, he placed his injured foot on the coffee table.

Shea was glad he was engrossed in the movie, it relieved some of the tension she felt around him.

She was secretly pleased he wanted her back at the station. She'd missed him today.

When the popcorn was finished, Jake moved the bowl to the side table and glanced at Shea.

"Thanks."

"Want more?" she asked.

"Nope, I'm good."

She nodded and turned back to the movie. But from the corner of her eye she could see Jake glancing her way from time to time.

He feigned watching the show, but as her heart rate increased, she doubted he was as caught up in the movie as he seemed.

Not that tonight was a date, but it almost felt like it. Who knew the Christmas cop could be interested in a quiet night at home?

When the movie ended, Shea switched off the TV.

"So did you like it?"

He nodded, glancing at his watch.

"I didn't realize how late it is. I'll be going. Thanks for the movie and popcorn. It's been a long time since I watched a movie."

"Anytime. There are lots of Christmas movies," she said.

Maybe he'd take her up on the suggested invitation and watch another one with her.

Jake put on his heavy jacket, picked up the cane and walked to the door. Shea moved past him to open the door. The cold air swirled in.

"I'm glad you came tonight," she said with a smile.

He studied her for a moment, then lowered his head slowly as if giving her time to withdraw before he kissed her again. His lips were warm against hers. In only a moment he dropped the cane and drew her into his arms. She came willingly. She didn't want the kiss to ever end.

Her heart raced, blood pounded in her veins and her internal heat sensor soared. She hugged him as hard as he hugged her. The kiss went on and on. It was heavenly.

The flash of headlights as a car turned into the complex penetrated the delightful sensations that encased her. The front door was wide open, letting in all the cold air and letting the light from the living room highlight the two of them. Slowly she pulled back.

"Good night," Jake said, scooping up his cane and heading for his car.

Sighing, she turned and entered her condo, closing the door behind her.

The night ended too soon for her.

She was doubly interested in going to the police station tomorrow. Who knew what the day would bring?

7

Shea was the first in the office the next morning. All her notes about Christmas were on her laptop, so she turned it on to review.

It wasn't long before she heard Jake in the hallway. Her heart sped up. She stared at the computer screen but didn't see what was right in front of her. She was totally attuned to Jake.

He entered and walked to the desk he was using.

She looked up and smiled.

"Good morning," she said.

"Ummm," he answered, his frown more pronounced than normal.

"Who rained on your parade?" she asked, surprised at his attitude.

He'd seemed friendly last night, what changed?

He looked at her and shook his head.

"Sorry, I've been thinking about that kid who came in. It's really cold out today and snow's predicted."

"Jason," she prompted.

He nodded.

"So, it's been cold all week, all month come to that."

"His jacket didn't fit very well," Jake said as he looked at the papers on his desk.

"So you want to get him a new jacket, get him one that fits and is super warm for this time of year," she guessed.

He nodded. He looked at her. "It's not quite the same as when I was a kid, but I think from where they live, money's tight. And a kid should have clothes that fit."

"So get him one from the Christmas list and give it to him early," she suggested.

"I haven't a clue what size to get. Nor what color he'd like."

"If it isn't to be a surprise, take him shopping and let him pick out what he wants."

He stared at her for a long moment. "Maybe."

"He'd probably love a shopping expedition with a cop."

He didn't reply, but began looking at papers in the folder in front of him.

Shea went back to reviewing the time line for the project. She was curious about the space at St. Anne's.

"I'm going to go to St. Anne's to check it out," she said after a few minutes.

Jake looked up. "Why?"

"To get a feel for the place. Don't you want to check it out so we have an idea of what it looks like before the wrapping party."

"Wrapping party?"

"I thought it more fun to call it a party than just gift wrapping. I figured we can have hot cider, pizza and cupcakes for everyone who helps. Did I tell you my entire staff has volunteered that night? And most of them want to help distribute."

"And how many is that?"

"Fifteen counting me and Cal. And so far all the volunteers I've talked to are planning to help again this year. It really is a great community effort."

He frowned again, closing the file folder.

"I'll come with you to St. Anne's. I haven't seen the place either."

"Didn't you help last year?" she asked.

He shook his head.

"I told you, I'm not much for kids."

Shea wondered if he'd change his mind as the project unfolded. He seemed to relate when Jason visited. Enough to want to do something for the boy now.

"Let's go. We can also check out some of the vendors after we see St. Anne's," Shea suggested. "I'll drive."

She could see Jake hesitate when she said that and she grinned.

"Afraid of a woman driver?"

"Not at all."

She suspected that was a lie, but didn't challenge him on it.

When they reached her car, Jake stopped in surprise.

"This is yours?" he asked, examining the smoky blue car with the wide white racing stripes down the middle.

Shea nodded, unlocking the doors with her key fob.

"It's a Shelby GT," Jake said admiring the car as he took in every inch of it.

"No wonder you're a detective. Nothing gets by you," she teased climbing into the driver's seat.

He got into the car a minute later and became fixated on all the features on the dashboard.

Shea grinned and started the engine. In only moments they were on the road heading to the church to check out the staging area.

"I guess being a geek pays pretty well," he said a moment later.

"Now. But for many years Cal and I struggled just to pay basic bills. And while I did indulge myself with this car, I also have savings and a retirement plan."

"It's a sweet ride," Jake murmured.

They stopped at the rectory for St. Anne's and met the priest, Father Damian, who was happy to show them the area they reserved for staging presents and wrapping them. The hall was spacious with racks of folded tables and chairs lining one wall.

"Plenty of seating for however many volunteers you have," Father Damian said. "Carolyn Warner is signing up volunteers from the church. She told me yesterday she has thirteen lined up so far for wrapping and five for delivery."

"Fantastic. We'll have so many volunteers we'll probably finish in record time," Shea said enthusiastically.

The priest reviewed how the process worked in previous years and both Shea and Jake were reassured that things would run smoothly with all the experienced people involved.

"Now to make sure we have the up-to-date information for the kids and their wish lists," Shea said.

"Carolyn's handled that from our end. She's been in contact with the other churches in the diocese and every one will have their list to her by next Sunday. She'll then send it directly to you," Father Damian explained.

"We're running ads on several social media sites both for donations and names of kids in need," Shea said.

"We are?" Jake asked.

She nodded. "It's not that big a deal, but it'll reach a lot of people in a short time."

They thanked the priest for taking time to show them around.

The next stop was Tots To Teens Toy store, the largest one in Mondano.

By the time they finished meeting with the manager of the toy store, it was lunch time.

"Want to head for Ben's?" Shea asked as they left the big box store.

"Sure."

"Want to drive?" she asked, holding out the keys.

Jake looked at her for a moment his eyes lighting up.

"What do you think?"

He reached out and she dropped the key in his hand.

In only moments they were on the road.

"If you want to swing by the interstate, you can open her up," Shea said. "Though as a police officer, I'm sure you'll obey all speed limits. This baby will do zero to sixty in 3.3 seconds."

He glanced at her and nodded. A quick right at the next light and they were heading out of town and toward the interstate.

"Are you always so generous letting practically strangers drive your car?"

"Not so much. Cal's taken it a few times. He loves it, but he's a dad and they have two practical mini vans. Steve at work's borrowed it a couple of times. He likes to show off when dating new women. It's just a car."

Jake didn't respond to that comment, but he loved the power he felt as he accelerated onto the freeway. She was right, it went up to sixty in no time. Pushing the car a bit faster, he was careful to stay just over the limit. He knew any cop in the area would be after them in a heartbeat if they saw this baby speeding along.

After ten minutes, he found a on-off ramp and headed back to town.

When they reached Ben's, Jake parked in the small parking lot.

"Thanks," he said, handing her the keys.

She grinned at him. "Fun, huh!"

"You have no idea."

They ate lunch at Ben's and reviewed the progress of the project.

Both felt better after having spoken with both the priest and the manager of the primary source of toys. There were other stores that donated toys, games and clothing. But for now, phone calls to touch base were all they planned to do.

Once back at the police station, Jake resumed his review of the cold case he'd been working on. He had an idea he wanted to explore. It might amount to nothing, but looking over the notes, he could see that a clue had been overlooked. Or at least not reported on.

He glanced over at Shea who was once again focused on her computer screen. He knew she was updating the lists.

For the first time he wasn't annoyed by being assigned this task for Christmas. He wouldn't have ever crossed paths with her if not for this project.

Not that knowing her changed anything.

Except--she intrigued him. She seemed to have a sunny optimistic outlook on everything. Which was totally opposite to his view of life.

She didn't have to help out. Her work on the police department's software program had ended. She could be doing a dozen other things.

He was glad she'd stayed.

Frowning, he rose. Time to stop thinking about Shea O'Riley. He wanted to check out that piece of evidence again. Then talk to his boss about bringing in the man he wanted to talk to so he could question him.

Shea suddenly jumped up and began walking around.

"I'm heading to evidence," he said as he rose and walked toward the door.

"I'll walk with you if I may," she said. "I need the steps and it beats walking in circles."

The evidence room was filled with shelves holding box after box of items kept concerning crimes.

The policeman in charge pulled the box Jake wanted. Shea peered into the box when he opened it and then wrinkled her nose and stepped back. There were bloody clothes in plastic bags. Her guess—a homicide.

Jake pulled out several plastic bags with names and dates and initials scrawled over them. Finally he pulled out one with a spiral bound notebook.

"I want to take this upstairs," he told the evidence cop.

"Sign here."

When they reached the elevator, Shea asked what he expected to find.

"There are discrepancies in a time line. This was the victim's journal. One of the detectives ten years ago jotted a note to compare times, but I never saw a follow up. So I'll see what I can discover. Maybe nothing. Maybe he did follow up and it led nowhere."

"Does he still work here? You could ask him."

"No. And I'm not sure where he is these days, so I can't ask him directly. I'm hoping I see the same discrepancies he did. It might require another interview with one of the suspects."

When they reached their office, Shea noticed it was snowing. She went to the window and watched for a minute while Jake sat at his desk.

"School will be out soon," she commented, turning back to face him.

He looked up. "So?"

"So let's see if Jason's mother will let him come with us to get a new jacket," she said.

Jake looked out the window, then tossed his pencil on the desk and rose.

"Fine with me. The storm's supposed to last a day or longer and dump several inches of snow."

"Do you remember his address?" she asked.

"I do."

When they arrived at the address Jason had given, Shea's heart dropped. It wasn't in a very pretty neighborhood—mostly other buildings. No grass she could see though every flat surface was already covered with a dusting of snow.

They walked inside, Shea keeping an eye on Jake with his cane. She didn't want him to slip on the snow.

When they reached the door to the Billingsley's apartment, Jake knocked.

Shea looked down the hall wondering which door led to Susie's home.

She turned back when she heard noise inside. But no one came to the door.

Jake knocked again.

Nothing.

"Tell them you're a cop," Shea said, putting her ear against the door. "I think I hear someone inside."

"It's the police," Jake said.

A moment later the door opened a crack. Then as far as the chain would allow.

"Hi," Shea said with a smile. "Remember us?"

Jason nodded. "I don't know anyone else who has pink hair."

"Is your mom at home?"

Jason looked at Jake and back to Shea. "I'm not supposed to tell," he said.

"Is she at work?" Jake asked.

Jason nodded.

"Where does she work?"

"At the diner. She brings us food home every day."

"Which diner?" Jake asked.

Jason pulled back a little and stared at him with wide eyes.

"If you tell me where she works, we can go there and ask her if it'd be okay for you to come shopping with us," Jake said.

"Shopping? For food?"

"Do you need food?" Shea asked, suddenly wondering the exact situation the family was in.

"Mom'll bring some home."

"Are you home alone?" Jake asked.

Shea reached out and touched his arm.

"Tell us where you mom works and we'll go ask her."

"Pete's diner. You can walk there. Mom walks there every day."

"Okay, we'll be back if your mom says it's

okay for you to come with us," Shea said, her hand still on Jake's arm.

They turned to head back down the stairs.

"He's too young to be home alone," Jake said.

"I know, but it sounds like they're doing the best they can. This apartment building doesn't exactly scream money. There isn't even an elevator."

When they reached the lobby, Shea pulled out her phone. "I'm searching for a Pete's diner, but nothing's coming up."

"Try something close by, maybe it goes by another name."

"There's one a couple of miles from here. It's called Eat and Go. Do you suppose that's the place. Not exactly what I think of as walking distance."

"Nothing else?"

She swiped her phone a few times and then shook her head. "Nothing even close."

"Let's try that."

The light snow drifted straight down. There was no wind, for which Shea was grateful.

When they arrived at the Eat and Go Diner, they went inside. It was a typical diner, red plastic covers on the benches in the booths. Chrome and red chairs for the tables and red seats on the stools by the counter.

There were few people inside.

"Can I help you?"

A woman who looked to be in her early thirties came over. She had on a pink dress uniform with a white apron over it. She looked tired.

"We're looking for Mrs. Billingsley," Shea said.

"I'm Carla Billingsley." She didn't even seem curious as to why two strangers would be asking for her.

"I'm Jake Morgan," he said pulling out his badge.

Her eyes widened. "Is something wrong? Is Jason okay?" A hint of panic sounded in her voice.

"He's fine. Though I wonder if he's old enough to be home alone."

8

"I'm Shea O'Riley," she said, interrupting. "We're working on the Mondano Police Department's Christmas project. We met Jason last week when he came to the station."

"I was shocked when I learned what he'd done. He knows better than that."

She looked at Jake. "He's home alone today because my babysitter and her kids came down with a bad cold and I didn't want him to be exposed. She checks on him every hour and then lets me know he's okay. Normally he isn't home alone."

"Is his sitter Susie's mom?" Shea asked.

Carla nodded.

"We wondered if it'd be okay with you if we take Jason shopping for a little while. He could help us with picking out presents for other kids. It helps to know what kids that age are really into these days," Shea said with a warm smile.

"I guess it'd be okay." Carla looked at Jake

and then back to Shea. "I'll call him and let him know."

"What time do you get off work?" Shea asked.

"Six o'clock," Carla answered.

"We'll have him home by then."

As they were leaving the diner, Jake frowned.

"I still think the kid is too young to be left at home without adult supervision."

"Maybe, but his sitter's just down the hall and what else do you expect a single mom to do? She has to work to earn money to keep that apartment. She sure can't bring him here."

"I could have child protective services—"

Before he could finish the sentence, Shea rounded on him, putting her hands on her hips.

"Don't interfere in something you don't know about."

"I do know about kids left alone and the trouble they can get into."

"Such as?"

"Vandalism, petty theft, even arson."

"Did you work with kids?"

He looked horrified. "No way."

Shea turned away so he couldn't see her smile at his response.

No wonder the cops at the station teased him about being this year's Christmas Cop, he must have made his views of kids known far and wide.

"Jason doesn't seem the type," she murmured as they continued to the car.

"You never know. I was in a group home that had some wild boys who looked like altar boys."

"But I doubt Jason's wild. He is respectful and honors his mothers instructions."

Jason was ready when they knocked on his door.

"Mom said I have to use my best manners. And I have to tell Naomi that I'm going. But Mom already told her so she knows it's okay."

Shea walked with Jason to the door three down from his apartment. As soon as he knocked, a young woman answered. Her dark hair looked lank, her eyes were watery and her nose was red from constant blowing. She didn't get too close but smiled at Shea.

"We're taking Jason shopping," Shea said.

"I recognized you from Carla's description. Thanks for taking him. He'll be good, he's a really great kid."

She smiled at Jason.

"I hope you feel better soon," Shea said stepping back a few inches. She didn't want to catch what Naomi had.

"Me too, and my kids. I'm hoping we're all well by Christmas."

Jason was excited to be going with Shea and Jake, though he tended to keep a wary eye on Jake. He was a little disappointed they weren't driving a police car.

Shea asked him about school and his friends and Susie. The boy was happy to chatter away answering all her questions as they drove to the store.

When they reached Tots To Teens Toy Store, Jason's eyes grew big.

"We're going in here?"

"We sure are. We need your help to see what kids your age want so we can tell Santa," Shea said as she parked near the entrance. Snow continued to fall, but so far the accumulation wasn't much.

Once inside Jason seemed overwhelmed.

Jake glanced around and looked at Shea.

"I had no idea there were these many toys for kids. How in the world do they focus in on one or two?"

"My guess is word of mouth. If one girl gets a special dolly, she tells her friends. Or if a boy gets a super hero and flaunts it to his friends, immediately they'll all want one. Let's see what Jason's drawn to."

They walked up and down the aisle, taking their time. Whenever Jason stopped to study a toy, Shea took a picture to add to their database of toys to get. They were learning the names of toys so they knew what to ask for when ordering.

When Jake realized how long it was going to take, he wasn't sure his ankle was going to hold up. He could already feel the ache growing.

Shea looked at him.

"Need a break?" she asked quietly.

He didn't want to admit to any weakness— especially in front of her, but common sense told him he could do more damage forcing the ankle beyond what was comfortable.

And that made him mad all over again with the situation.

She pulled out her keys and handed them to him.

"Wait for us in the car. We'll be along soon."

He wanted to protest, but couldn't. Taking them gratefully, he looked at Jason. "Watch out for Shea."

The boy visibly puffed up with pride that the policeman trusted him to watch out for her.

Shea gave Jake a wink and started down the next aisle with Jason.

Jake leaned heavily on the cane as he walked back to the flashy car. He admired it again.

Shea continually surprised him. He didn't know why a woman with pink hair wouldn't be drawn to a Mustang. What did he expect her to drive?

Glad to get off his feet, he pushed the seat back as far as it would go and stretched out his aching leg. He acknowledged he wasn't the best patient in the world. He wanted to be back to normal and back in the field.

Not looking at toys and supervising a Christmas program.

And if his partner didn't stop teasing him about it, pay back was coming sooner than he expected.

He had Shea to help and for that he was grateful. What would it be like to work together on other projects?

Like nothing. They had nothing in common except for Christmas. She'd help out here and then be gone. Unless the computer program had another glitch.

When Shea and Jason returned to the car, Jake was downright cold. He hadn't turned on the heater and was glad when she started the engine.

"It's freezing in here, why didn't you have the heater on?" she asked as she backed the car out of the slot.

"Didn't want to run down the battery or waste gas," he replied. "A little cold never hurt anyone."

"One more stop and then ice cream!" Shea said.

"One more?" Jake asked.

She gave him a sideways look and nodded. "As a reward for helping us out, we'll see about a jacket for Jason."

"A new jacket?" the boy asked from the back seat.

"You look like you're out growing the one you have on," she said.

Jake liked the way she presented the new jacket—so the kid wouldn't think it was charity. He remembered when he'd been a child and donations had always made him angry that he didn't have a family like other kids, that he was a charity case.

The department store was close by and in a short time they were in the boys department. As they passed the shoe display, Jake glanced at Jason's shoes. He could use a new pair that was obvious.

He stopped. The other two stopped and looked at him.

"What?" Shea asked.

"I'm thinking a new pair of shoes."

Jason looked between the two of them, then at the display of running shoes in front of them.

Jake looked at Shea, then at Jason.

"I believe his help was really good. So two things would be a good reward."

Jake felt a kick in the chest when Jason smiled widely. His eyes lit up and he looked so hopeful Jake suddenly wanted to do everything he could to keep that bright hope alive for the kid.

"You're right," Shea immediately agreed.

Jason was a happy child when they walked into the ice cream shop a half hour later. It was close to dinner time, but Jake figured ice cream wouldn't slow the appetite of a growing boy.

"This has been the best day," Jason said when they were seated at a small table, each with their own flavor ice cream in front of them.

Jake nodded, realizing it hadn't gone as badly as he'd expected. He glanced at Shea who was smiling at Jason. For a moment, the world was golden. He'd never have experienced this if he hadn't broken his ankle. Maybe every cloud did have a silver lining.

After they took Jason home, Shea asked Jake where she could drop him.

"Want to go for dinner? I know a good Mexican place."

"Sure. I love Mexican. Where to?"

Jake was glad the afternoon wasn't coming to an end yet. He liked being with Shea. She was different from other women he knew. And the pink hair was growing on him.

Dinner conversation centered around the Christmas project. They reviewed the plans for contacting everyone, for delivery of the donated toys and clothing.

"You know," Shea said at one point. "I wonder about Jason's Christmas Day dinner."

"What about it?"

"What if they can't have turkey or ham and all the trimmings? What if it's just another catch as catch can meal? Of if his mother has to work that day and only gets to bring home left overs from the diner?"

He studied her for a moment.

"Are you suggesting we now include a Christmas dinner for every one? There are now one hundred and forty names on our list."

"I know, but some of those are multiple kids in a single household. I bet we wouldn't need more than maybe eighty-five dinners."

"Eighty-five dinners?" he repeated.

She nodded. "I've been thinking about it, and I figure we can contact a bunch of stores and ask if they'd donate a ham or a turkey. Maybe some cranberry sauce, potatoes, rolls, you know all the things that go into a Christmas dinner. And pie for dessert. If we ask a bunch, each could donate just a few. It'd be great."

He nodded slowly, entranced at her enthusiasm.

"It'd be great all right. Except it adds another aspect to the project and we're still not sure we have the toys angle covered. How large are the families? How many really need this?"

She shrugged. "It doesn't matter. We'll give enough for a large family and if they have left overs, all the better. And my guess is kids on your list are from a poor home or why would they be on the list? I can get some help from the employees of our company. We'll have to coordinate those donations with the toys, and make sure they get to St. Anne's the afternoon we're delivering, but early enough to put with the toys for each house.

Jake closed his eyes for a second, imaging the chaos at St. Anne's. Then he looked at her and smiled slowly. If anyone could pull it off, it'd be Shea.

"I'm officially putting you in charge of the dinners," he said.

She grinned. "It'll be awesome, you'll see."

Shea drove Jake to the police station after dinner to get his car. Jake wished he'd asked her to drive him home. Then he could have invited her up for a drink.

Instead, he'd go home to his empty apartment and she'd go home to the Christmas extravaganza in her own place.

He knew where he'd rather go this evening.

"So I'll see you in the morning?" he asked as he opened the car door.

"Yes, I'll be there bright and early and ready to start calling grocery stores. And check in with St. Anne's to make sure we can put perishables in a refrigerator until delivery time. Oh, and we'll need boxes or bags or something to carry the food." She smiled brightly at him. "I'm glad you included me in this project," she said.

Jake nodded and climbed out of the car. If she only knew how glad he was!

The next morning Jake arrived at the make-shift office to find Shea already at her desk, on the phone. She waved at him and continued to talk. From what he could hear, she was already talking some grocery store into food donations.

He sat at his desk and looked at the folder he'd left yesterday. He'd asked the lieutenant to see about having a patrol officer bring in one of the suspects from the original investigation. He'd found information in the journal that contradicted the suspect's statement. He wanted clarification.

"Woohoo," Shea said, turning to face him. "Good morning. I have great news. Three stores so far have volunteered five dinners each. That's already fifteen and I have only called three. If everyone gets on board, we'll have enough for all the families."

"Good job."

"Do you want to go with me back to St. Anne's? I want to check out refrigeration possibilities."

"I have someone coming in this morning. If you wait until after I interview him, I'll go with you."

"A suspect?"

"Let's just say a person of interest."

"From one of your cold cases."

He nodded.

"Can I watch the interview? I'd love to see you in action."

He shook his head. "No, you can't."

"Okay. Tell me how it goes," she said, turning back to the phone.

Jake considered her request. He'd rarely had anyone beyond fellow cops to talk to about his job. Sometimes it was interesting, sometimes dangerous, and sometimes tedious. Did she think being a cop was glamorous? Television portrayed crime as easily solved in sixty minutes. This case he was working on was still open eleven years after the murder.

He hoped he'd have some good news to share when the interview was over.

9

Shea was pleased with the results of her calls. Jake still hadn't returned from interviewing his person of interest and she'd already lined up 90 donations for Christmas dinner.

And talked with Cal about asking their employees if they'd help pick up the donations. Unlike the toys that were being delivered, the grocery stores required them to pick up the food.

Still, no worries about things going bad if they picked them up and then delivered within a short time.

Shea heard Jake as he walked down the hall. She was about ready to head out for lunch and would see if he wanted anything.

He carried the folder he'd left with earlier.

"So, how did it go?" she asked.

"We made an arrest," he said. The note of satisfaction was evident in his voice.

"Just from that one interview?"

"Yes. Once I presented the facts as I saw

them and outlined the rest of the follow-up, the man confessed."

"Wow, that's unexpected."

"I was surprised as well. Only thing I can think of is the guilt's been weighing on him for all these years and he just wanted to come clean."

"What happens next?"

"The D.A.'s been apprised and his office takes it from here."

"So you solved it. One of the cold cases. That's so cool."

Jake shrugged. Dropping the folder on the desk, he sat down.

"I'm about ready to go get a burger. Want the usual?" she asked, jumping up and putting on her jacket.

"Sounds good." He reached for his wallet, but she waved it away.

"We can settle up later. I'll be back soon."

Shea was glad for the break even though it was still frigid outside with a steady wind blowing that made it seem even colder. She bought their lunches and hurried back before the cold air cooled their food.

Jake's lieutenant was sitting on the edge of the desk next to his, talking with Jake when Shea entered.

"Oops, should I wait outside?" she asked, pausing in the door way.

"No, come on in. We're just about finished," the lieutenant said. "I see you brought lunch. I'll leave it to you both. Good job, again, Jake. I knew if anyone could find something it'd be you."

The man smiled at Shea and left the room.

She brought their lunches to Jake's desk and deposited the drinks and bag. Shrugging out of her jacket, she dragged one of the chairs closer and reached for the burger he handed her.

"Atta boy from the boss—that's cool," she said before she began to eat.

"Better than hearing I screwed up," he said dryly.

"Do you screw up often?" she asked, a teasing light in her eyes.

"Not if I can help it. Not sure how the ankle fits into that, though."

"Since you didn't break it deliberately, it can't be a screw up. Are you going to delve into another cold case now?"

"Contrary to what everyone seems to think around here, that is what I'm supposed to be doing while on desk duty. Not Christmas stuff."

She grinned. "Ah, but the Christmas Cop project is so much fun."

"Not so much if that's all your coworkers call you now."

"At least you don't have to play Santa Clause to a room full of kids."

He frowned. "Okay, so I'll count my blessings."

Shortly after they finished eating, Phil came in to congratulate Jake on solving the case. He was the first of several other officers who stopped by during the afternoon to talk about the case and congratulate him.

Shea watched, warmed by the camaraderie the police officers shared. She noted everyone seemed to hold him in high regard and was pleased the others took time to say something to him.

She suspected it'd help him be more resigned to desk work until he was fit to return to active duty.

Cal called about mid afternoon.

"Can you stop by the office before going home?" he asked.

"Sure. Is there a problem?"

"Maybe on the Furston project. Several of us have been looking at it all day and are going crazy. I'm hoping you'll spot something we've missed."

"I can leave now and be there in twenty minutes."

Jake looked at her when she hung up.

"Problem?"

"Sounds like it. I'm needed back at the office." Once she put on her jacket, she gathered her laptop and backpack and started out.

"I don't know if I'll be back today or not. Depends on what I find," she said by the doorway.

He acknowledged her comment, but didn't say anything further.

She wished he'd said something about hoping she'd return.

Tomorrow was Saturday. She didn't work Saturdays unless it was critical. So she wouldn't see Jake again until Monday. She hesitated at the door, but didn't know what to say.

"See ya," she called and headed for her car.

The problem the entire company had been working on was critical enough that Shea went to work on Saturday. The review the evening before proved the custom program wasn't working as they'd projected and all hands were needed to try to find the problem. She'd stayed until after eleven the night before and was in before anyone else that morning.

Cal stopped at her door, coffee cup in hand. "Find anything?"

"No, and it's so frustrating."

"You don't have to tell us. We've been looking at it for days. I'm almost at the point I want to say start over, but that'd take weeks. We need to find the glitch and fix it. The rest of the crew will be in shortly."

"It's totally frustrating. And this is the second one if we count the problem with the police department," she said, eyes still on the code. "Has Esther been doing double checks at each stage?"

"Of course. It was merging all the different aspects that led to the problem. Are you going back to the cop shop?"

"Not until we get this solved."

Cal smiled. "It's good to have you back with us," he said.

She looked up and smiled at him.

"It's good to be back. I think I can do most of what I need to do for the Christmas project from here. Guess you're stuck with me from now on."

"Works for me." He lifted his cup in silent salute and headed for his own office.

Nothing was resolved on Saturday and Shea took Sunday off to catch up on chores around her home.

Monday the entire team was back to work trying to find the problem with the program before they came up against their deadline.

It was almost lunch time when Shea's phone rang.

"I take it you're not coming in today," Jake said after greeting her.

"No. In fact this problem may take longer than we think and I might not be there the rest of the week. Is that a problem?"

"No. I believe things are on track."

"I think so, too. If anything comes up, call me."

"Right."

Shea felt a little disappointed she wouldn't be seeing Jake for a few days.

Since when had he become so important to her? She gazed off into space for a few minutes, wishing she could handle the review at the police department and not be stuck in her own office.

She shook her head. What was she thinking? She and Cal had built up a strong company, one she loved and was proud of.

She'd only known Jake for a few days, how had he become so important? Something to think about when she had time. Now she wanted to find out why the program wasn't working the way it was designed to do.

Jake hung up the phone disappointed he confirmed his suspicions. He'd suspected she wouldn't be in. She never arrived so late.

But he didn't like the idea she might not show up for days.

Not that she needed to. He was lucky to have had her help with the Christmas project as long as he'd had it. It was his project, thanks to his boss. If he needed help, there was an entire police department to tap.

Looking around the empty office, he missed her. The entire room seemed more empty than normal. He checked his watch. Would she be up and wandering around getting her steps about now? Or, more likely, heading out for lunch somewhere.

Today he'd make do with the vending machine choices. Then get back to work on this new cold case. The investigation looked to have been very light as if there was little intent in solving it. He didn't recognize the name of the detective in charge. Gone before he started, Jake guessed.

But the information didn't hold his attention like it should.

He kept glancing at the empty desk Shea normally used.

Shea, Cal and four of their programmers were watching the large screen as one of the programmers slowly scrolled through the code.

"Here's where we brought in the subroutine," Esther said pausing the screen so everyone could study it.

"Looks clean," Cal said.

The others murmured agreement.

"Then the next one was down a bit," she said, slowly scrolling the code so everyone could quickly scan it as they moved through the program.

"Wait, hold there a second," Shea said. She frowned as she studied the information on the screen.

"That might be it," Cal said.

The others leaned forward to better see.

"Because of that?" one programmer pointed to the line.

"Yep."

Shea noticed someone entering the large space. She looked over.

"Jake," she said, jumping up and going over to him.

"Hi. What are you doing here? Is there a problem?" she asked when she got close.

"Not a problem, I wanted to update you on some information that came in this afternoon. So I thought I'd take the chance you were still here."

Everyone by the large screen had turned when Shea left and were staring at them.

She glanced back.

"Come on and I'll introduce you around and then we can go to my office."

She led the way and once by the group, quickly made introductions.

"Sorry to interrupt," Jake said.

"No worries, I think we know where the problem is," Cal said. "Thanks to Shea's eagle eyes."

"Then I'll leave it to everyone," she said, turning toward her office.

Jake fell into step with her. "Was that the problem keeping you here?"

"Yep and if that's the only glitch, once it's fixed we'll try the entire program again.

Sometimes the tiniest thing can bring the whole thing crashing down."

She entered her office and gestured to a chair. She took the one next to it and smiled at him, surprised at how happy she was to see him.

"Something that couldn't wait?" she asked as he sat in the next chair and held on to the cane.

He shrugged, looking around, taking in the awards hanging on her walls, the desk cluttered with printouts, and the two large screens on either side of the desk.

"I thought you'd have something fancier than this," he said.

She grinned.

"We have a very fancy conference room where we usually meet with clients--to give the image of a highly successful firm. The rest is utilitarian. Good enough for us."

"I got a call from station KZFF about doing an interview about the Christmas project."

"Cool. That's great publicity. It will make sure a lot of people know about the program. If you have a website or something, folks could donate directly to that and help fund costs. Gives the public a feeling of being involved."

He frowned. "I don't want to go on television. But if my lieutenant finds out, I'm a goner."

She grinned. "You need to think of the kids. Actually, this might even turn up more kids who wouldn't have Christmas if not for the Christmas Cop."

"Great, just what we need, more kids."

"Ah, but you'll probably get more volunteers, too. And if you give a shout out to those donating things, you'll engender a lot of good will and maybe spike sales for those who are donating."

He frowned. "I wanted you to help me think of a reason not to do it, not come up with all these ideas making it sound like a good thing," he grumbled.

She laughed, reached out and patted his arm.

"You'll have to practice a smile, however. Your usual demeanor scares kids."

He frowned even more.

Shea laughed again. "So maybe you need something to light up your world."

"Like what?" he asked.

"I don't know. What do you like? What hobbies do you have?"

"Searching cold cases?" he offered.

"Like that's a hobby. Do you like fishing, painting, model railroads?"

He shook his head.

"So what would your best day look like?" she asked.

"Riding my bike through the mountains in the fall when the leaves change."

"You have a bike?"

"A Harley."

"Wow. I didn't know that. Will you take me riding sometime?"

"Sure." His expression softened. "Once my ankle's better and there's no snow on the roads."

She narrowed her eyes. "Do you belong to a motorcycle club?"

He shook his head. "Mostly I like the freedom and the solitude. I'm around people all the time with work, I don't need more on my off time."

"Too bad. I was thinking Bikers for Christmas. Well, maybe another time. At least you aren't frowning as much as before."

He looked at her for a long moment. "I know something that would make me smile," he said softly.

"What?"

"Another kiss."

10

Shea felt the heat rise in her cheeks as her heart rate sped up. She stared into his eyes for a long moment, then gave into temptation and leaned over so her lips brushed against his.

She pulled back and stared into his eyes.

Slowly Jake began to smile.

She laughed. "So that's all it takes for a smile?" she asked.

"Guess so."

"I'll keep it in mind. Now, when is the TV interview? We want them to have a trailer across the bottom giving the website and where people can donate or recommend kids for the program."

"I'm not committed yet."

She ignored his comment. She knew when the chips were down, he'd come through.

"I'm going to call Stan at your IT department and talk about another page on the police website. This could really expand the program throughout the city."

"Sounds like more work to me," he grumbled.

"We'll have it so automated there will be very little work to do," she said, rising to cross to her desk. In only a minute she was scribbling ideas and notes on paper.

"There might be a limit to how many toys a store will donate."

"That's why we want the general public to donate money, so we can buy what isn't donated," she said, focused on the ideas already crowding in her mind.

"We could discuss it over dinner," he suggested.

She looked up at that and grinned. "I'd love it. What do you have in mind?"

"What are you up for?"

"How about we go back to my place and order in pizza. We can work from there and won't have to worry about others around us."

He nodded. "Sounds good."

Before they left, however, Shea called the police department's IT section and talked with Stan. Getting his okay to draft up a page, she smiled. "I'll have something for you tomorrow," she ended.

"That's done," she said.

Jake enjoyed watching her enthusiasm. She

jumped right in, and knowing what she was doing, was able to start the ball rolling. Now he felt more obligated to make that appearance on KZFF, much to his chagrin.

They ordered pizza before leaving Shea's business, knowing it'd cut the wait time at her condo. They only beat the delivery by ten minutes.

Jake was again amazed at the way her place was decorated. She had enough items to open her own Christmas store.

"So did you solve any more cases today?" Shea asked when they were seated and began to eat the pizza.

"No, but I did delve deeper into another murder. This one seems to have been investigated thoroughly. Sometimes, however, things turn up later that put a different slant on things."

"Like?" she asked.

He wasn't sure she really wanted to know, but her trait of focusing solely on the person talking was enchanting. He liked her focus on him.

"Someone who benefited from the crime but didn't obviously do so at the time might lead to another round of questioning. And sometimes people let slip something they didn't reveal in the initial investigation."

"Umm. Does it ever get you down? You're always trying to find out what human killed another human. Wouldn't you rather do something else?"

"Like what?" he asked.

She thought for a moment, then shrugged.

"I guess every crime is pretty bad when I think about it. Maybe robbery wouldn't be so bad–then I think of an older person who has their entire life savings stolen, that's heartbreaking. Or juvenile cases–trying to get kids on the right track before they do something awful and then having them fail."

"It does get me down sometimes. Especially if it's a horrible crime. But I feel cops are the only hope left to see justice done for the victim. Even if there's no family left, or friends, at least I know I did what I could for someone who can no longer do for himself."

She smiled slyly. "So that's why you should do the Christmas project annually–have one time of year when you are surrounded by happiness, not death and destruction."

"Only I'm not good around kids."

"I wouldn't say that. You did great with Jason."

"That was one kid."

"Ah, it's bunches of kids together that get to you," she said.

"Maybe. I'm not usually around bunches of kids."

"Still, this is a great project and I think you'll find come January that it wasn't so bad and be psyched up next December to take charge again."

"Maybe. Would you jump in and help?"

She nodded her smile doing weird things to his heart.

They finished the pizza. Shea cleared the table and suggested they move to the sofa to complete their list.

She brought out her laptop and fooled around with different images and ideas, ending up with one she shared with Jake.

"What do you think of this for our page on the police website?" she asked, turning the laptop toward him.

"Looks good. I can't believe you put it all together in such a short time."

"Easy peasy. I'll send it to Stan and he can upload it to the department's website if he approves it. So expect calls to start coming in as soon as he gets it uploaded."

"I'll warn Janey. I'll check with the captain, but I think she could screen the calls. There are a couple of other support staff there who could help if we get swamped."

"Sounds like a plan. And a lot can respond by email that can be read when we have time."

She closed the laptop and half turned on the sofa to face him.

"So tell me more about the case you're working on. At least what you can tell me."

He talked with her for a while about the cases, the frustration with being so long after the fact, and the variety of reports–some well done, some virtually useless.

"So does the police department review these cold cases only when someone has desk duty?" she asked.

"We used to have a couple of guys devoted to cold cases, but budget cuts eliminated those positions, so yeah, pretty much when someone like me is on disability but can still man a desk."

"Seems sad that the crimes are never solved. I'm glad you caught one bad guy at least."

"I still have several more weeks on the DL. Maybe I'll find something on another case."

"Want to watch a movie?" Shea asked. "I've got more Christmas movies we can watch."

"To get me in the mood for the holiday?" he asked.

She nodded. "Pump us up for the big day, and all the excitement those kids are going to have when we start showing up at their doors with presents and Christmas dinner."

"You look almost as excited as you're saying those kids will be," he said.

"No more frowns. This is the best time of year!"

She selected *Miracle on 34th Street* and whipped up a batch of popcorn. They sat in companionable silence watching the story unfold.

Shea had tears in her eyes at the ending. "I love this movie," she said.

She looked at Jake. He looked at her.

"Didn't you say that about the other one we watched?"

She nodded. "Probably, I love all the Christmas movies. Did you like it?"

He shrugged. "A little too sweet. Life isn't always that way."

"Which makes the movie special because you can actually believe it might be that way sometimes. You're cynical because of your job."

"Or you're an idealist because I haven't a clue why. No hardships in life, maybe?"

"Maybe, or because I choose to see the best. Want any hot chocolate before you go?"

"No, but thanks for the offer. With your problem at work solved, will you be coming to headquarters tomorrow?"

"Yep, I'll be there."

Shea walked him to the door and waited patiently while he put on his heavy jacket.

She wasn't planning on a goodnight kiss, but if Jake wanted one, she was game.

He did.

Shea dropped her things at her desk at the Mondano Police Department the next morning and took her laptop up to the IT department. After some discussion with Stan and, a quick call to the chief of police, the web page for Christmas was approved. Working together it took only a short time to have it up and operational.

"I still think we should have a picture of Jake wearing a Santa hat on the front page," Stan said.

"I can just see that–not," Shea replied.

She grinned just thinking about Jake and the Santa hat.

Jake didn't like the teasing he got from the others, he'd hate to have his face on the website, no matter how good the cause.

She grabbed her laptop and headed back to

the large room she shared with Jake. He was at his desk, papers spread all around, on the phone arguing with someone.

She waved and went to sit at her desk. She planned to check in with volunteers this morning and set up a feed from the website Christmas page directly to a report so they could quickly gather data for kids in need and donations.

Jake slammed down the phone. "Stupid bureaucracy," he said.

"Obviously a problem."

"About the TV interview. My captain wants me to do it, but now the public affairs department wants to coach me on what I can and cannot say. I know enough to focus all attention on the Christmas project. What do they think? I'm going to give away some crucial information about an ongoing case?"

Shea leaned back in her chair and let him vent. She didn't see much of a problem, but Jake was obviously wound up about it.

"Can you get a list of the questions before you go?" she asked.

He looked at her. "Probably."

"Then get the list, send a copy to whoever's bugging you and prepare to answer the questions without giving away any crucial information on a murder case."

She smiled at the thought. Even she knew Jake would never do such a thing.

He rubbed his face in frustration. "I don't have time for this. I want to focus on this case."

"Remember this is for the kids."

"The new motto–for the kids," he grumbled.

She nodded. "Good news, we have the website page up for the project, got the okay from your captain, and I'm setting up a spreadsheet for the information we'll get. You need to give the studio the links so they can have the trailer across the bottom ready to go when you're interviewed."

He nodded and reached for the phone again.

In only a minute, Shea heard him ask for Sara Stanton, the afternoon anchor who'd be doing the interview. He explained what he wanted and listened to her apparently tell him how to handle things. When he finished the call, he looked at Shea.

"She's going to email me the questions and I can email her back with the website info."

"Okay, let me know when you get the email and I'll give you the URL."

A few minutes later Shea was caught up in contacting volunteers and verifying schedules for wrapping and for delivery.

When her watch indicated time to walk, she

jumped up and started to roam around the room. Noting that Jake seemed intent on what he was reading, she took her walk in the hallway instead.

They were a week away from the wrapping party. She'd double checked all her lists and contacts. Every thing looked to be coming along perfectly. She hoped so. She was so excited for the kids to have a taste of Christmas she was almost fearful about thinking how well it was going. She didn't want to jinx it.

"Are you taking a break for lunch?" Jake asked some time later.

She looked up. "I am. Want the usual?"

He nodded, holding up some bills.

Shea was glad for the break, though it was cold outside. And it looked like more snow might be in the works. But the fresh air cleared her head. And she had lunch with Jake to look forward to.

She loved spending time with him. His seriousness was in direct contrast to her own more lighthearted view of life. She was definitely an optimist. He leaned toward the pessimistic side, but if she had to deal with the horrors he did, she might feel that way, too.

It was fun to be part of a couple. Not that they were a couple, necessarily. But they did watch movies together, eat together, work together.

She liked the idea of a possible future with Jake.

Would they continue to see each other once the project was behind them? She'd be back at her office, he'd get off the disabled list and return to work.

She knew from the talk she'd picked up around the department that most of the detectives didn't keep strict nine to five hours. If interviews needed to be done in the evenings, they were right there.

Still, he'd definitely not work all the time.

She hoped they'd continue to see each other. She was starting to think she wanted more than just a few hours here and there. She'd like to see where this attraction led.

Did he feel the same?

11

"You do know I have another job," Shea said as they were finishing lunch.

Jake looked at her and nodded. "Your point?"

"I need to get back to work. My work. This is fun, and I can keep checking for updates, but we're closing down over the holidays and I want to get as much wrapped up before then as possible on some of our projects."

"The TV interview is Thursday," he said. "Can you stay until then?"

"You don't need me. I can give you an update right before you go on the air if you need it. Did you get the questions?"

"Yeah, and they're easy, mainly explaining what we do, asking for names of any kids we might not know about and asking for donations."

"You'll remember to smile, right?" she teased.

"Do you not have any faith in me?"

"Of course I do, only sometimes I think you forget that."

He faked a grin at her and she burst out laughing.

"Okay, maybe a bit tamer."

She went to her desk and picked up a scrap of paper.

"Here's the URL for the web page. It's easy to remember. Really all anyone has to do is log onto the police website and hunt for Christmas."

"I'd expect people who see the broadcast will respond that afternoon, don't you think?" Jake asked. "Maybe you could be here then to make sure everything's working like you want for gathering the data."

"Sure. That'll work. So I'll take off after we finish lunch and be back Thursday afternoon."

"How about dinner tomorrow night—just last minute coaching for my big television debut."

"I'd like that. Where can I meet you?"

"What would you like, we've done Chinese and Mexican and pizza. The basic food groups."

"How about Rusty's Steak House. They have melt in your mouth filet mignon."

"Six o'clock?"

"Deal. I'll look forward to it."

She knew she'd miss being here at the cop shop as Cal called it. But she had her own responsibilities, too. And she'd better remember that. No matter what happened in the future, she knew this project was ending in a little over a week.

They were ramping up as the holiday drew closer. Next up was the television interview. She expected a lot of input from that. Then next Tuesday was the wrapping party and then all hands on deck with picking up the meals and delivering everything. It ought to be a total madhouse that day at St. Anne's, but she trusted it would all work out as it had in previous years.

Wednesday Shea had a hard time concentrating. She was looking forward to dinner with Jake and found herself daydreaming when she should have been reviewing code. Or imagining a celebration dinner on Christmas for a project that exceeded expectations when she should have been reviewing financial numbers.

She could hardly wait for dinner.

Cal came in around 4:30 and sat in her visitor's chair.

"I think everyone's getting short-timer's disease."

"What?"

"There's more conversation going on about Christmas and presents and the kids deliveries than there is discussing program plans."

Shea nodded. "I'm having trouble concentrating myself. Well Christmas is just over a week away. We had this last year, as I remember."

"I almost feel like shutting down now, but we still have six more days and we can get some work done."

"Nothing major I expect," she said, tossing her pencil down and leaned back in her chair. "I'm fine with just coasting for these next few days. When everyone gets back in January, we'll all be rested and focused on the new projects and customers."

"I know. I'm as bad as the rest of them. I'm taking off now. You staying?"

"For a while. I have a date at six, so will go directly there from here."

"With the cop?" Cal asked.

She nodded.

"You two are close," he said.

"We're working on the project together."

"Is that all? No conversations that aren't project related? No activities that aren't project centered?"

She shrugged. "We've been to dinner a couple of times and watched some Christmas movies."

Cal studied her for a moment, then jumped

up. "Take care of yourself, Shea. Have fun tonight."

He gave a slight wave and left.

Shea checked her watch and decided she'd call it a day as well. She had time to go home and change from jeans to something nicer for the steak house.

Not that she was dressing up for a date. Though she'd called it that with Cal.

Was it a date? Of a kind, she thought.

And she never looked forward like this to a business meeting.

It was promptly at six that Jake entered Rusty's Steak House. The hostess greeted him and he'd hardly finished saying he was meeting someone when Shea entered behind him.

"We're ready," he said to the hostess after greeting Shea.

She led the way to the quiet table near the side. The restaurant was sparsely occupied. No one sat at the tables near theirs.

He helped Shea take off her coat, surprised to see the silky white blouse she wore. Noticing further she was dressed up—not the usual jeans and T-shirt she normally wore.

"You look nice," he said as he sat opposite her and hooked the cane on the back of the empty chair.

"Thank you. It's the Christmas season, I thought I'd dress up a bit."

She smiled brightly and then looked at the waiter when he brought the menus.

"I already know what I want," she murmured, leaving the menu closed.

"Filet mignon, I remember," Jake said. He glanced at the menu and then gave their order.

"So are you nervous about tomorrow?" she asked.

"Not especially. I've given testimonies in court, so I figure this won't be as bad."

She laughed. "I hope not. You had the questions ahead of time and the TV station is supporting the project, not like they are trying to trip you up."

"True. How are things going at your work?" he asked.

"Slow."

She told him about the lack of focus and interest as they drew closer to the holidays.

"We don't see much of that at the station," Jake said. "Mostly because so few of us have Christmas Day off. This'll be my first one off in a long time."

"You're still coming over, right?"

"Yes, around ten you said."

He was looking forward to spending time with Shea with nothing to worry about–no cold cases, no Christmas for kids. Just the two of them sharing a holiday together.

She nodded.

"So tell me," Jake said after their meals had been placed in front of them. "How did you end up here in Mondano when your family isn't from here. From what you've said you're close to your family."

"Cal's from here. My folks moved to Florida as soon as I graduated from high school. They waited so I could finish out my schooling. I'm the youngest, the rest of my brothers and sister had already moved out. So while I do have siblings and cousins and grandparents still in my hometown, I felt no strong pull to return with my parents gone."

"So you and Cal decided to open your business here? Not Silicon Valley in California?"

"Cal's parents are still here, and it's not that far from the eastern part of the state. I can visit after only a few hours' drive. So it seemed like a good idea. Now we've been here seven years, and our company's grown a lot."

"So no plans to relocate?"

"Not for me. I love it here. I like the changing seasons, the friendly people, the church I attend. Our company's like a family almost. We're close to our employees and each other," she finished, taking a bite of her filet.

"Oh, this is so good," she said with a smile on her face.

Jake enjoyed his steak as well, without quite the obvious swooning that Shea had no problem demonstrating.

He was glad to see her enjoying her meal. Occasionally in the past he'd dated women who were on strict diets, which made it hard to find a restaurant they'd both enjoy.

Dating? Were he and Shea dating?

This would count as a date. Especially when their conversation veered to the personal instead of staying completely on topic of the Christmas project.

He liked the idea. He liked Shea. She was easy to talk to, fun to be around. And pushed him a bit outside his comfort zone.

He never thought he'd be looking forward to the happiness he expected now on the faces of the kids when they delivered the presents. He remembered Jason's expressions when he got the new shoes and new jacket.

Jake had yearned for something like that when he'd been a kid. Only he never got it. Maybe there was something to this philanthropic project. He'd been too focused on criminal behavior and investigations in the past.

He would never have asked for this assignment. But now he wasn't as upset with his lieutenant as he had been.

"So what do you remember about your parents?" Shea asked.

"Not a lot."

For the next few minutes—and with prompting from Shea--he searched his mind for the few elusive memories he had.

"So the moral of that is to always have a plan in place in case you die young," he ended up.

"Or be born into a family with lots of siblings, aunts and uncles and long time family friends who could step in and take over if a couple ends up gone before their time," she said.

He nodded. How would his life had gone if his parents hadn't died? Or if he'd had a slew of relatives around to take him on? To share family values and stories.

What did he have to pass on to his kids?

Whoa. He stared at his empty plate. Kids? He hadn't ever thought about getting married and having kids. Glancing at Shea, he was glad she couldn't read minds.

Was being with her giving him ideas?

"I'll have the creme brulee for dessert," Shea said as she slid her plate a little bit away from her. "That was delicious, but I still have room for dessert."

They ordered coffee and dessert. Even after the creme brulee was gone, they lingered in conversation.

Finally Shea looked around.

"Yikes, we're like the only ones still here."

Jake followed her gaze and noted only one other table still had customers.

"Guess it's time to go."

She nodded. "You need your rest, your big television debut is tomorrow."

"Thanks for reminding me."

She grinned. "We'll be watching," she said as Jake signaled the waiter.

He walked her to her car.

"Thanks for dinner. I had a great time," she said as she unlocked the door.

"I did, too," he said.

Once the door was unlocked, he turned her back to him and kissed her. The kiss went on for several delightful seconds.

Jake wished he'd picked her up so he could take her home. And be invited inside. Maybe another time.

"Good night," she said breathlessly a minute later.

Jake watched her leave the parking lot before he limped to his car.

Promptly at one the next afternoon, Shea had the large screen television at work tuned to KZFF. The others in the group wandered over to watch as well.

After a brief introduction by Sara Stanton, she introduced Jake.

He looked terrific, Shea thought.

"Wow, he looks as good there as he does in person," Esther said.

Shea turned the volume up a bit.

"So tell us about the Mondano Police Department's Christmas program," Sara said.

Along the bottom of the screen a trailer scrolled from right to left with the web page link clearly displayed.

The interview went well. Sara asked all the questions she'd provided Jake beforehand. At the conclusion, she urged city residents to join in and make this a special Christmas for all the children in Mondano.

"Your guy did good," Cal said at the end when Sara introduced her next guest.

Shea turned off the TV.

"I hope we got a lot of response. The station really covered it well."

"We're all looking forward to the wrapping party and delivering the gifts," Esther said.

"When you see some child's face light up, you'll be so happy you volunteered," Shea replied. "My heart melted when we bought a jacket for Jason. He was beyond happy."

Shea finished a couple of tasks she had going, then headed for police headquarters. She was too impatient to see the web response to wait until Friday.

Hurrying to her desk at police HQ she was happy to see Jake had obviously just returned. He was shrugging out of his jacket.

"You did great!" she said, hurrying over to his desk and giving him a big hug.

He smiled. "It went well. Are you here to see if we have any response yet?"

"I am. And it'll air again this evening and even more people will see it then," Shea said.

She took off her jacket and booted up the computer at her desk.

"Oh, this is so cool. There are eighty responses so far."

She downloaded the responses to an excel file and then printed copies for both of them.

Taking one to Jake, she brought hers and sat at his desk.

"So new kids here. Not too many. I need to cross check with our list to make sure they aren't already on it. And some new volunteers. We can call them this afternoon while they're still really enthusiastic."

Jake looked at the files on the side of his desk. "Guess they'll have to wait a little longer."

"I know they're important, but this is, too, and it'll all be over soon."

"You know I get my cast off on Tuesday."

"Will you be returning to active duty then?" she asked.

"Not until the doctor declares me fit. I have a little physical therapy to endure to make sure everything's up to speed."

They began making calls.

An hour later Janey came into their room with a pile of papers.

"The phone is ringing off the hook with volunteers offering to help, or send money, or send toys. Marcie's helping. I couldn't keep up with it all. Here's what we've gotten so far."

She handed the stack to Shea.

Janey looked at Jake. "And we got a couple of callers asking how to reach you. You're a star."

He scowled at her comment. "No star, just hoping for more for the kids."

"This year's Christmas Cop is doing better than Harry ever did," Janey said as she left the room.

"You'll probably be the Christmas Cop for the foreseeable future if this goes smoothly," Shea said in a teasing tone.

"Unless someone else gets on the DL next year and I can foist it off on him."

Shea was delighted with the response from the general public. She couldn't wait for delivery day to see the kids she'd deliver to and watch as they realize what's happening. She cherished the memory of Jason when he got his shoes and jacket.

It was after six when Jake looked up. "Want to grab a bite to eat?" he asked.

Shea finished her note and looked at him. Checking her watch, she nodded. "Yeah. I'm getting blurry eyed cross checking all these. And after seven I'm expecting another flurry of responses on the web."

"We can get to them tomorrow," Jake said. "This has been a long day."

"Let's go back to my place and order in. I feel like kicking off my shoes and really relaxing," Shea said.

"I'll follow you over."

When they reached Shea's condo, Jake was again amazed at the festive feel to her living room. He remembered a scrawny tree at the home. And sometimes there'd be presents, but as he recalled they were often for the younger kids.

"Want to start a fire?" she asked when they'd taken off their jackets.

He nodded.

"I'll call for dinner. What sounds good to you?"

"I don't much care. Anything you want is fine with me."

"Well, you're easy. How about pot roast? The cafe near here has take out. I can order and then zip out to get it."

"Or I can go. Sounds good."

Jake went to the fireplace. There was a small stack of wood to one side. He laid the wood and then used one of the long matches to light it. In only a couple of minutes a small fire began to generate some warmth.

Shea finished ordering and turned with a smile.

"Thanks. That'll be cozy tonight. I'm glad it's only cold and not snowing again."

He joined her on the sofa.

"In fifteen minutes, I'll zip out to get dinner," she said, relaxing, shoes already off. She tucked her legs under her and gazed at the fire.

"This is nice. I don't have a fireplace at my apartment."

"It was one of the requirements for me when looking for a place. We had one growing up and I remember all the winter holidays we'd all gather in the living room with a fire roaring and lots of laughter and fun. My mom said she misses it in Florida, but it's never cold enough where they live to use one."

They ate dinner in front of the warm fire. It had begun to snow again, but the storm was not supposed to bring more than a trace.

When the food had been procured and divvied up, they sat on the sofa. When he began to eat, Jake looked at her television. "Do you have another Christmas movie to watch?"

"Always. How about *Holiday Inn?* It's for more than Christmas, but a winner."

He shrugged. "I've watched more movies since I met you than I have in the last five years."

"Don't get out much, do you," she said with a smile.

"Usually working, or grabbing as much sleep as I can with the hours I work."

"Too much work isn't good for anyone."

"Maybe."

They finished eating and Shea found the movie. They sat side by side on the sofa, Jake's foot on the coffee table. Shea brought a lap robe to cover their legs and scooted closer to Jake. She relaxed when the movie started. Tonight was turning out to be a wonderful night.

12

Tuesday morning Shea arrived at St. Anne's at ten o'clock. The parking lot was already half full.

The cold spell continued and Shea wore her heaviest jacket and a knit stocking cap to keep warm. Once they began deliveries, she'd be in and out of her car.

She relished the warmth of the hall when she entered.

Toys had been delivered and were staged on long tables along the side wall by category. The volunteers already present were preparing long trestle tables with wrapping paper, scissors, tape and tags. Shea had the master list and Jake also had a copy.

"Ready to start?" Father Damian asked greeting her.

"As we'll ever be, I think. Did any of the food arrive yet?"

"Some of the canned goods arrived yesterday.

We have the kitchen all set up to receive the cold foods and Betsy has the list of families. As soon as we have volunteers for the food detail, we'll start boxing and bagging meals to be ready to go when the presents are."

"Wow, I'm amazed at all the toys. I know we have almost 150 kids, but the number of toys is overwhelming."

"You'll see, this runs pretty smoothly. We've been doing it for seven years, remember. This is just your first time."

She nodded. "Has Jake arrived?"

"I haven't seen him. But some of the police from the station are over by the coffee. Help yourself to a cup. The Alter League also put out donuts."

"Sounds good, thanks."

Shea put her clipboard and backpack by a chair at the wrapping tables. She glanced around and was pleased to note things did seem to be coming together in some sort of order. She hoped it would continue.

Walking over to the coffee station, she recognized a couple of the cops standing around talking. She hadn't had much to do with any of them beyond the ones in IT and the lieutenant. And Jake.

She wondered if she could slip in between them to the coffee urn and get a cup.

"Naw, Jake's not the type," one of the men was saying.

Shea stopped when she heard his name. She kept her head down. What was he not the type of?

"So you don't think he's interested?" another asked.

"With some geeky pink hair programmer? Are you nuts? He's just using her for help for this project. As soon as that cast comes off, he'll be back at work and I guarantee you we'll never see the pink hair wonder again."

Shea caught her breath. She knew she should move away. Or make herself known, or something. But she felt glued to the spot.

"I've seen women Jake's dated. They're nothing like her."

"They spend a lot of time together."

"It's for the project, guaranteed."

She spun around and walked back to her backpack, blinking back tears.

Was the cop right? Had Jake spent time with her just because of the project? She knew she'd been helpful and that he'd railed against the task in the beginning.

But all the evenings they'd spent together had

to count for something.

She saw Jake enter the large hall. Her first impulse was to march over to him and ask him if what his coworker had said was true.

But what if it was true? What if he said so?

She turned back to the table, taking off her jacket and stocking cap and putting them on the back of the chair. She grabbed her clip board and headed for the toys.

Jake joined her a couple of minutes later.

"Father Damian said there's coffee," he said walking up beside her. He was using his cane but she noticed his walking cast was off.

"So you've graduated," she said, looking at his foot.

"Still feel a bit wobbly. It came off this morning. And I have more exercises that I knew would strengthen ankles. But I'm almost back where I hope to be. We ready for this?"

"I hope so. Let the games begin."

Before long volunteers lined up to get the individual sheets that listed households. Kids, toys, food and all were on the sheets. Once everything was wrapped, packaged together and checked off, the items went to the door where volunteers who were delivering packages awaited.

The air was festive. The hall was filled with laughter and conversation and Christmas carols playing softly in the background.

Shortly after noon, pizza was delivered with enough pie to feed all who were present, plus those delivering the gifts. Volunteers took turns eating. When those delivering presents returned for another batch, they quickly ate.

It was after one when Cal and the crew from their company showed up.

"We're ready to roll," he said when he found Shea elbow deep in wrapping presents.

"I'm going to switch off to delivery now. I've been wrapping a gazillion toys, between checking the progress of the wrapping and the food deliveries and all the others tasks. I figure delivery will be a nice change."

"We're ready," Cal said looking eagerly at the activity.

Shea greeted her employees and soon handed out instructions.

"So when you get a check list, double check everything you're loading. And don't get different households mixed up. Everything should be labeled. If you have any questions find me or Betsy or Jake." She pointed to Betsy and Jake so they'd know who to look for.

She put on her jacket and drew on her cap. "Is it still cold out?"

"Really freezing. And the wind's kicked up," Cal said.

Shea fell in line behind another volunteer and soon had her items for delivery. She had three households which lived near each other. Verifying she had what she needed, she headed out. She packed her car, making several trips, and then punched in the first address on her GPS.

The mother at the first house opened the door.

"Ho, ho, ho, delivery for Avery and April," Shea said. "Straight from Santa. He couldn't make it so he sent me."

The two little girls were totally awestruck, especially when several wrapped presents were brought in. The mother was most grateful for the presents and totally surprised by the Christmas dinner.

"I had no idea we'd have a special dinner, too," she said. "This is so wonderful. I had no idea."

"Merry Christmas," Shea said with a bright smile. Her heart was happy at the delight she witnessed. This was such a wonderful project. She was glad she was part of it this year.

The next house appeared empty when Shea knocked. She waited a few minutes, not sure what to do. She didn't want to leave the presents outside. Yet she didn't want the kids to miss out. She was about to return to her car when a car stopped behind her and four little children tumbled out.

"Is it Christmas?" the older boy asked racing up the walk way, his eyes fixed on the stack of wrapped boxes Shea was holding.

She gave her Santa-sent-me speech and smiled at the kids who were jumping around in happiness. The mother smiled at them and Shea.

"Thank you for waiting. I was afraid I wouldn't make it back in time to be here, but we had a doctor's appointment that ran a little late. These look amazing. You can tell they are so excited."

She unlocked the door and ushered in the children. "Remember, these are for Christmas Day, not now."

"Oh, mom," they groaned.

Shea had to make three trips for this house, but she left knowing this family would have an amazing Christmas.

It was mid afternoon by the time she returned for another load. It had gotten even colder, Shea believed. She was happy to be temporarily inside the large church hall.

"Jake's looking for you," Stan said as he passed with a stack of presents to be wrapped.

"Thanks."

She wasn't sure she wanted to see Jake right now. She was too conscious of the comments from his coworkers.

"Hey, Shea, Jake's looking for you," another cop called out.

She nodded and looked around the large area. The toys stacked on the tables on the side were greatly reduced. The wrapping tables still held the paper supply looking somewhat diminished.

She went to get another load for delivery and ran right into Jake.

"I've been looking for you," he said.

"I just got back from deliveries. And I'm getting ready to deliver a bunch more."

"Want a ride along?" he asked.

"I can manage," she said.

"I wouldn't be much help. I delivered some but my ankle's really bothering me. Enough I needed to take some of the pain meds the doctor gave me. So no driving. I tried wrapping, but I'm all thumbs. So pretty much all I can do is keep you company."

She considered her options. Despite the hurtful words she heard earlier, she wanted to be with Jake. She hesitated another minute then nodded.

"Can you help load up my car?" she asked.

"Another couple of trips and then I'm going to have to cave."

"Come on then. With you in the car, I can leave the motor on and keep it warm. It's really cold out."

The second part of the afternoon was a repeat of the first part. Shea delivered presents and meals and enjoyed the wide-eyed wonder of the children, and the grateful, sometimes tearful, appreciation of parents.

She was delighted to see they had Jason's gifts in their pile.

"How did that happen?" she murmured when she noted the name and address.

"I flagged it when I first arrived this morning. I'll even go up with you for that one."

Shea gathered up the food bags and some of the presents, Jake took the others, cane in one hand.

They trudged up the stairs in silence. Shea couldn't help replaying the conversation she'd overheard this morning. Had Jake only spent time with her so she'd help with the Christmas project?

They reached Jason's apartment and knocked.

Carla opened it and smiled. "Hi, I'm happy to see you. Jason's down at my neighbor's. Come on in."

"If we sneak in and out, you can hide the presents until Christmas morning if you want," Shea said. "Some families are letting their children open the presents early, others are making them wait. I think it'd be hard to wait knowing they were here."

"I could do that. Are your bringing things for Naomi as well?"

Jake nodded.

"Bring her stuff here, too. That way all the kids will be surprised. I'll take the food over to her later when the kids are occupied."

"Sounds like a plan," Jake said.

When they reached the car, Shea suggested she take the other things up, so he didn't strain his ankle. She could tell looking at him it was giving him fits. It took two more trips to deliver all the presents and food to Carla. Then she returned to the car.

They returned to St. Anne's both reflecting on the happiness of Jason's mom and how excited she was to surprise her son on Christmas Day.

When they reached the church, the parking lot was almost empty.

"We might not be needed for another delivery," Shea said as they walked to the building.

Entering a moment later, she was surprised at the change. All the presents were gone. The tables were in the process of being folded and stacked away by volunteers. Another couple of people were sweeping the floor. She didn't see Cal or others from her company.

Betsy came over to them. "The last delivery left about ten minutes ago. We are finished for another year! The policemen said they'd clean up so I'm about ready to leave."

"Terrific," Shea said with a smile. "Is there anything I can do?"

The other woman shook her head. "It was a delight to be a part of this for another year."

Jake thanked Betsy for her help and went to talk with Phil who was folding the legs of a table.

"I think the cops have it. They did a fantastic job this year. You did, too. It's the largest we've ever done. I'm tired," Betsy said, but she gave a warm smile.

"Me, too. Thank you for your help, Betsy. You make everything run smoothly from this end."

The woman gave Shea a hug and wished her a merry Christmas. Once she left, Shea looked for Jake.

His back was to her as he talked with Phil. While she watched, two more men joined them. In only a moment they were all laughing.

"Merry Christmas," she said softly.

Turning, Shea went back to her car and headed for home. The let down was to be expected. They'd been gearing up for this day for weeks, now it was over and no deadlines loomed. Her company was closed until the new year. Cal would be on his way to his in-laws for the holiday.

She had the next few days off as long as no customers called with a problem. She could finish baking all the goodies she liked for the holidays. Visit with her neighbor before she left for her gift to herself—a week in Hawaii.

She wondered if she'd hear from Jake. She half expected him to call to say he wasn't coming Christmas morning after all.

The next day, Shea refused to let herself get down, she'd keep busy, and pushed away the echo of the men saying Jake only spent time with her for the help she could give.

She remembered every minute together—from working in the squad room, to dinners together, to watching movies. And every single kiss.

She was going to miss him more than any other person if he really wasn't going to continue seeing her.

Maybe she should change her hair color back to its natural blonde state.

No, she wasn't changing herself to conform to someone else's idea of what was normal. She was who she was and if others couldn't accept that, then they weren't meant to be part of her life.

She wanted to be loved for herself.

Whoa–love? Where had that come from?

She was in the midst of baking gingerbread cookies when the thought popped into her mind.

She stopped stirring and gazed off into space.

Love Jake? No. She was fascinated by him. Enjoyed hearing more and more about him. Laughed with him, shared special moments. And would be devastated if he never came by again.

But love? Wasn't it too soon to think such a thing? Just because she couldn't stop thinking about him, always wanted to share things with him, longed to see him didn't mean it was love.

That was something that grew over time, dating and spending time together.

The certainty grew that love was exactly the feelings she had for her grumpy, injured, solemn cop.

"Oh, boy, now I'm in trouble," she whispered.

13

Christmas morning dawned bright and sunny. The temperature was below freezing and the snow that had fallen earlier that week sparkled in the bright sunshine.

She began preparations for her day. She made beignet mix and brewed coffee. She wasn't sure if Jake would show up. He hadn't called since she last saw him at St. Anne's. But that didn't necessarily mean anything. Just a minor blip of disappointment that he hadn't called. It had only been two days.

She planned to put the ham in the oven soon. The side dishes and dessert she'd already prepared. They just needed to be warmed up when time to eat. That let her be as free as possible during the day.

Her parents called and they had a lovely chat. They were delighted to be in the warmth of Florida when they heard of the cold snap in Mondano. The call lasted almost a half hour, and when they hung up, Shea made a few other calls to grandparents, brothers and a favorite cousin.

She was getting hungry and was about ready to start frying the beignets when the knock sounded at the door.

Her heart rate increased and happiness bloomed. He'd come after all.

She opened the door with a big smile on her face.

"Merry Christmas!" she said.

"Merry Christmas to you," Jake replied.

In his hand was a bottle of wine and a wrapped box. He handed both to her as he stepped inside.

She took the items but before she could turn away, he leaned over and kissed her. His eyes were warm as they gazed into hers a moment later.

"You're just in time. I'm getting ready to make the beignets," she said, feeling flustered with the kiss. She wanted to drop the presents and wrap her arms around him and never let go, but thought that might be a bit over the top. She still remembered what was said at the wrap party.

She put the present beneath the small tree near the fireplace.

Jake looked around her apartment as he took off his jacket. He wasn't expecting much walking today so left his cane in the car.

On the fireplace hung two stockings. He stared at them. He hadn't seen them before.

"One for each of us, but we can't see what's in them until after we eat breakfast. Are you hungry?"

He tore his gaze away from the stockings, a curious feeling deep within. He tried to remember if he'd ever had a Christmas stocking before. He couldn't remember a single time.

"You got me a stocking?" he asked following her to the kitchen.

"Those are from Santa," she said, gathering the things she needed to make the beignets.

"So Santa just dropped down your chimney last night and left them?"

"Must have. I didn't have a fire yesterday. Didn't want him to get sooty."

He leaned against the counter to watch her cook. When she had a plate stacked high with warm beignets covered in powered sugar, she smiled at him.

"The coffee's ready and these are hot. Let's go in the dining area so we don't get sugar everywhere."

Jake felt as if he were in another dimension. One far away from crime and criminal elements.

The warm French doughnuts were delicious.

And Shea'd been right, it was hard to keep the powered sugar from getting all over everything.

She laughed as she brushed the white powder off her jeans. "I should wear white when eating these, but I never do."

"They're delicious. I don't think I've had them before."

"On my first trip to New Orleans I fell in love with them. I'd have eaten every meal at the Cafe du Monde, but the people I went with objected. Still, I whip up a batch now and then to satisfy my sweet tooth."

"Call me next time and I'll help you devour them," he said.

She looked at him. That didn't sound like a man who was not planning to continue seeing her now that the Christmas Cop project was over. Hope blossomed.

When they finished, she quickly cleaned up and then put the ham in the oven.

"We have a couple of hours until lunch. Shall we open presents?"

He nodded. He wanted to do whatever she wanted to do. He hoped the gift he'd brought was suitable. He had doubts, but Phil assured him it was appropriate.

She went to the mantel and unhooked the two stockings, handing one to Jake.

"Thank you or thank Santa. I've never had one before," he murmured as he sat on the sofa with the bulging stocking in hand.

"Stick with me, kid, and you'll have one every year," Shea said as she sat beside him.

"I'd like to."

She looked at him. "Like to what?"

"Stick with you."

Shea stared at him. Her heart rate increased. Her breathing became more erratic.

Jake gazed back at her, his eyes never wavering.

"Some of the cops at the wrapping said you only spent time with me because of the project and the help I offered."

"Some cops are dumber than dirt," he replied.

Slowly Shea began to smile.

"So you might spend some time with me apart from the Christmas project?"

He put his stocking on the coffee table, his eyes never leaving her.

"If I could have anything and everything I wanted, I'd choose to spend as much time with you as there is time," he said slowly, clearly stating each word as if to insure there was no mis-communication.

"You brighten my days. Expose me to a

whole other world I've never experienced. I didn't want this assignment, but you made it one of the best things I've ever done. You were with me every step of the way. And it turned out to be more rewarding than anything else."

"And fun, too," she said in a soft voice, her hands clutching her stocking.

"I hope we went beyond the project," he said.

She nodded. "I hope so."

"Enough to keep seeing each other?"

She nodded. Hope blossoming again.

"Enough to be exclusive?"

"Exclusive?" her response was squeaked out.

"I think I've fallen in love with you Shea. You are not like anyone I've ever known. This seems fast, but I think about you all the time. Count the minutes until I can talk to you again, see you again. Lie awake at night thinking about you."

She licked her lips. "I don't think it's too fast."

He reached out for her stocking and put it on the coffee table next to his.

"You don't?"

She shook her head. "I think I've fallen in love with you. At least my symptoms sound the same as yours."

He didn't wait for her to say more, but pulled her onto his lap and kissed her.

14

Sometime later Shea snuggled against him, staring dreamily into the fire.

"I'm thinking long term," he said.

"I am, too."

"As in marriage?"

She nodded, the smile threatening to split her face.

"So if I asked you today, you'd say yes?" he asked.

She nodded.

"Shea O'Riley would you do me the honor of becoming my wife?"

She looked up at him. "I'd love to and the honor is all mine!"

He kissed her at that.

The oven ding sounded and Shea reluctantly jumped up to see to the ham.

"It's almost time to get things ready for dinner," she said checking the oven. "Do you want to help?"

"I'm not much of a cook," he said coming into the kitchen.

"Lucky for you all we have to do is warm things up in the microwave."

"Ah, then it's lucky all around, I'm an expert with the microwave."

They prepared the meal together, sharing memories of Christmas meals past. Shea had long held family traditions, while Jake spoke of visiting Phil's family a couple of times before he stopped going.

They ate again in the dining area. Once finished, they elected to delay dessert until later as both were full from the meal.

"So time for presents now?" he asked. "I suspect once we open them, we'll be watching a movie."

She grinned and nodded. "One of the best, *White Christmas*. You'll love it."

Shea had stuffed his stocking with practical things like razors and batteries and an orange in the toe.

He held up the orange. "Do you think I need more vitamin C?" he asked.

"That's a long time O'Riley family tradition. Back in the day when my great grandmother was a girl, oranges were priceless. So my family saved up so each child could have one in his or her Christmas stocking. Now we can get oranges by the box full if we want. But the family tradition holds.

He nodded. "I'll remember that each year. Nice tradition."

She unloaded hers, also with practical gifts, including a new hair brush and comb. "My folks sent this. My mom still thinks I need to be surprised for Christmas."

She reached beneath the tree and pulled out a square wrapped box and handed it to him.

"Merry Christmas, Jake."

"Thank you." He opened it. A pair of warm leather motorcycle gloves.

"These are great! I can really use them."

"Once the roads are safe for a motorcycle," she warned.

He rose and handed her the gift he'd brought.

She opened the long box and lifted out the gold locket on a gold chain.

"It's lovely," she said studying it in delight.

"It opens for pictures," he said.

She pried it open. Two pictures could fit inside.

"So I'll do one of you and me, to celebrate our first Christmas together," she said, leaning over to kiss him.

"I like the sound of that—our first Christmas."

"The first of a gazillion, I hope," Shea said happily. "But none will be as special as this one. I love you, Jake Morgan."

"I love you, Shea O'Riley, and always will."

That vow was sealed with a kiss.

Did you enjoy this story?
If so you may enjoy **A Soldier's Christmas**

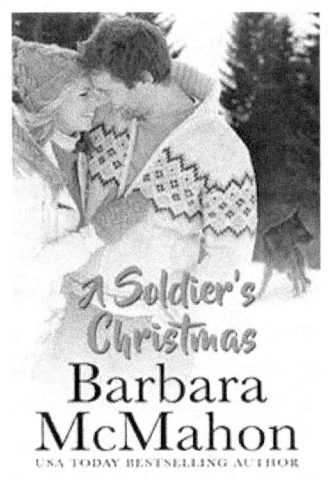

If you enjoyed **The Christmas Cop,** please
consider leaving a review.

For a complete list of Barbara's books, please visit
www.barbaramcmahon.com.

Lovecraft's Daughter

Amber LaShea Geislinger

The Morrigan Publishing

ISBN: 0615710794
ISBN-13: 978-0615710792
The Morrigan Publishing

www.morriganpublishing.com
www.lovecraftsdaughter.com

First Edition